ELLA

SID COLIN

THE LIFE AND TIMES OF
ELLA FITZGERALD

ELM TREE BOOKS
London

ELM TREE BOOKS

Penguin Books Ltd, 27 Wrights Lane, London W8 5TZ (Publishing & Editorial)
and Harmondsworth, Middlesex, England (Distribution & Warehouse)
Viking Penguin Inc., 40 West 23rd Street, New York, New York 10010, U.S.A.
Penguin Books Australia Ltd, Ringwood, Victoria, Australia
Penguin Books Canada Limited, 2801 John Street, Markham, Ontario, Canada L3R 1
Penguin Books (N.Z.) Ltd, 182–190 Wairau Road, Auckland 10, New Zealand

First published in Great Britain 1987 by
Elm Tree Books/Hamish Hamilton Ltd
Copyright © 1986 by Sid Colin

Reprinted 1987

British Library Cataloguing-in-Publication Data

Colin, Sid
Ella.
1. Fitzgerald, Ella   2. Singers—United States—Biography
I. Title
784.5   ML420.F52

ISBN 0–241–11754–2

Printed and bound in Great Britain by
Butler & Tanner Ltd, Frome and London

For my daughters:
Amanda, Lucy and Claudia

ACKNOWLEDGMENTS

I am indebted to many people for their help during the writing of this book. Among them André Previn, for his thoughts about working with Ella; Leonard Feather for his expert knowledge of all matters musical, and Judith Bronowski in Los Angeles, for her many hours of leg work.

My thanks to Sue Steward who did the research for both the book and the illustrations, and to Matthew Wright of Ray's Jazz Shop, who helped with the discography.

Thanks also to John Chilton, Peter Clayton, Peter Dean, Sally Feldman of the BBC, Audrey Franklyn of the Franklyn Agency in L.A., Dave Gelly, Kitty Grime and Nat Hentoff; to Tony Shoppee for his Down Beat archives, to Dave Howling, librarian at the Melody Maker, and Richard Saunders, Hilary Cole and John Grigg at Graphicom Express.

To the many authors listed in the bibliography, for many hours of pleasurable reading and for their expertise, my gratitude.

Sid Colin, London, 1985

The author and publishers would like to thank the following for permission to use copyright photographs in this book: Frank Driggs Collection (p. 1–3); Jazz Music Books (p. 4 – top picture) the Max Jones Collection p. 5 – both pictures; Rex Features (p. 4 bottom picture; p. 14); David Redfern (p. 6; p. 11 – bottom picture; p. 16); *New Musical Express* (p. 7; p. 8; p. 11 – top picture); Popperfoto (p. 9); Universal Pictorial Press (p. 10); The Photo Source (p. 12); Raymond Ross (p. 15 – top picture); The Press Association (p. 15 – bottom picture). Thanks also to *Melody Maker* for the use of their files.

Lyrics from the following songs are reproduced courtesy of Chappell Music: 'Who Cares? (So Long As You Care For Me)' © 1931 New World Music Corporation; 'Someone To Watch Over Me' © 1926 Harms Inc (Warner Bros Music); 'They Can't Take That Away From Me' © 1937 Gershwin Publishing Corporation; 'Oh Lady Be Good' © 1924 Harms Inc (Warner Bros Music) all composed by George Gershwin and written by Ira Gershwin, British publisher Chappell Music Ltd. 'I Get A Kick Out You' by Cole Porter © 1934 Harms Inc (Warner Bros Music); 'How High The Moon', composed by Morgan Lewis and written by Nancy Hamilton © 1940 Chappell & Co Inc., 'The Object Of My Affection' by Pinky Tomlin, Coy Poe and Jimmie Grier © 1934 Irving Berlin Inc., assigned to Bourne Inc.; 'Five O'Clock Whistle' by Josef Joe Myrow, Kin Gannon and Gene Irwin © 1940 Advanced Music Corporation, British publisher Chappell Music Ltd. 'Sing You Sinners' by Sam Coslow and Franke W. Harling © 1930 Famous Music Corporation; Mr Paganini by Sam Coslow, © 1936 Famous Music Corporation, British publisher Famous Chappell.

'Goodnight My Love' by Mack Gordon and Harry Revel, 'You Showed Me The Way' by Chick Webb, Teddy McRae and Ella Fitzgerald (1937) and 'A-Tisket, A-Tasket' by Al Feldman and Ella Fitzgerald are reproduced courtesy of Big Three Music/CBS Songs Ltd; 'My Buddy' by Gus Kahn and Walter Donaldson (1922) courtesy of Francis, Day & Hunter/EMI Music; 'Gulf Coast Blues' by Clarence

Williams, 'Into Each Life Some Rain Must Fall' by A. Roberts and D. Fisher, 'Stone Cold Dead In De Market' by Wilmouth Houdini (1934) courtesy of MCA Music; 'Judy' by Hoagy Carmichael courtesy of Campbell Connelly; 'Shine' by Ford T. Dabney, Cecil Mackey and Lew Brown (1937) courtesy of ATV Music (Lawrence Wright catalogue).

Amateur Night at the Harlem Opera House was always a rowdy affair. The auditorium was packed to the doors with connoisseurs of the performing arts, assembled to pass judgement on anybody with the nerve, the sheer iron-clad gall, to stand up there on the stage and face them. Show wise and hyper-critical, this crowd had seen 'em all: the hoofers, the Lindy-hoppers, the ballroom smoothies; the blues shouters, the Bing Crosby sound-alikes, the bathroom divas, the stand-up comics, the cigar-box jugglers, the paper tearers, the harmonica blowers. Yes, they'd seen 'em all, and to all they had delivered their considered verdict, more often than not in the form of a resounding Bronx cheer, and for the once hopeful, now defeated performer, the long lonely walk back to the wings, and oblivion. Oh yes, they used to say: if you can make it in Harlem, baby, you can make it anywhere.

On this particular night in 1934, the lamb about to be led to the slaughter was a sixteen-year-old girl, tall for her age, with awkward arms, and, as she would say in years to come, 'the skinniest legs you've ever seen'. When she made her entrance that night, those legs were shaking so much she could scarcely walk. The audience began to giggle, and there were a few cat-calls. 'Hey, honey, where'd you get them clothes?' She was indeed a strange sight. She wore an ill-fitting dress, shoes which were clearly intended for somebody else, and her unruly black hair looked as if no comb would ever master it. In the glare of the spotlight, she stood transfixed, frozen to the spot.

The Master of Ceremonies consulted his list. 'Okay folks, the next contestant is a young lady named Ella Fitzgerald,

1

and she comes all the way from Yonkers.' Well, that was good for a laugh, and the audience obliged.

> Who cares
> If the sky
> Cares to fall in the sea?
> Who cares if banks fail in Yonkers,
> 'Long as you've got
> A kiss that conquers.

Many years later, Ella would include that song in her *George and Ira Gershwin Songbook*, and people would say, well that's it, that's the definitive version.

'Miss Fitzgerald here is gonna dance for us, right? Hold it, hold it. Now what's your problem, honey?'

Ella was in urgent, whispered consultation with the M.C. The audience was loving it. They laughed some more.

'You what? Just a minute. Okay, folks, do you wanna hold it down just a little out there? Thank you. Okay. Correction, folks. Miss Fitzgerald has changed her mind. She's not gonna dance, she's gonna sing. Sing what, honey? "The Object of my Affection". Great song. Okay, she's gonna sing "The Object of my Affection". What key? She doesn't know what key. It doesn't *matter* what key.' He turns in mock despair to the pianist. 'You happy, Professor? Well let's get this show on the road. Sing, honey.'

So Ella sang. Imagine the terror of that moment. She had meant to dance, but the thought of it had turned her knees to water. At least, when you sing, you can hang on to the microphone, stand like a shipwrecked mariner in mountainous seas. Even so, it was only slightly less of an ordeal. And what was she doing there, anyway? She was there on a bet. Two of her school friends had drawn straws to see which of them would dare go up there on the stage and do something on Amateur Night, and Ella had drawn the short straw. So here she was. And in the Roman Circus atmosphere of the Harlem Opera House (thumbs up, thumbs down), who knew which way the wind might blow, hot or cold?

2

She sang a song she had learned from a Connee Boswell record. The song was somebody else's, but the voice was Ella's: clear and true, sweet and golden.

> The object of my affection
> Can change my complexion
> From white to rosy red;
> Any time you hold my hand,
> And tell me that you're mine.

The critics listened. They liked what they heard. Give them their due, when they liked something, they would roar their approval and raise the roof. They wanted more, so she sang them 'Judy', another Connee Boswell song. This one written by Hoagy Carmichael, the man who had recently given the jazz repertoire one of its most enduring standards, 'Stardust'.

> She's the one for me,
> Heaven sent her to be
> My Judy,
> My Judy.
> She's as sweet as pie,
> And I know that I'd die
> For Judy,
> My Judy....

Ella remembers: 'Three encores later, I had the twenty-five dollar first prize.'

By an extraordinary coincidence, on that very night, another girl was paying her first visit to Harlem. She came from Ella's home town and was born within a month of her. She too wanted to take part in the contest at the Harlem Opera House, but finding herself too late, had gone to the newly opened Apollo Theatre, had entered there, and won. Her name was Pearl Bailey, and in her book, *The Raw Pearl*, she wrote: 'I'm grateful I didn't go down the street to the Opera House. I doubt I would have made it there, for that night a young girl walked on stage, opened her mouth, and the audience that had started to snicker ended up cheering.

3

The girl sang "Judy". Her name was Ella Fitzgerald. She won, and that voice will go down in history.'

Harlem is that part of New York City which begins at Central Park, stretches north to 155th Street, west to Morningside Drive and east to the East River. By 1932, its inhabitants were, as near as no matter, exclusively black. A city within a city.

But it had not always been so. Until 1900, Harlem had been an all-white neighbourhood. A place of broad avenues bordered by fine houses and stately apartment blocks. People who lived there in those days remember it with affection. Richard Rodgers was born at number three, West 120th Street, a brownstone stoop house at the corner of Mount Morris Park, 'one of the prettiest little parks in New York'. They remember its quiet elegance; can recall strolling along Seventh Avenue on Saturday mornings in top hat and frock coat, and, after dark, arriving by carriage at Hartig and Seaman's Music Hall on West 125th Street to see Fanny Brice, or at that same Harlem Opera House with its gilded foyer, there to see Henry Irving in *The Bells*, or the musical shows imported from London, *San Toy* and *The Geisha*.

Until 1914, those theatres were out of bounds to blacks; and even after that, they were only allowed in the balcony, or, as they called it with bitter humour, 'nigger heaven'.

As the black invasion continued, the outraged white residents stubbornly resisted it. They formed protective associations pledging themselves never to sell their property to blacks. They were defeated, and for two reasons. One was that Manhattan's long established negro population was being hounded out of its old neighbourhoods downtown: Hell's Kitchen, between 34th and West 42nd Street (there had been a race riot of epic proportions down there in 1900), and the Tenderloin, on the West Side between Seventh and Eighth Avenues from 31st to 33rd Street. There the Pennsylvania Railway had flattened everything to build its new

4

station, and, as the *New York Herald* reported in 1903: 'The Tenderloin, that famous landmark of vice and blackmail, has passed into history.'

The other reason was the building boom of 1898 to 1904, when property developers had built prodigiously following news that a subway tunnel was to be driven beneath Lenox Avenue, and had then failed to attract enough white customers to fill their new houses and apartment blocks. To them it seemed a splendid idea to invite the black refugees from the West Side to occupy them, incidentally charging them far higher rents than they ever charged their white tenants. The blacks paid up willingly. They were moving from squalid slums to the best housing they had ever enjoyed.

The news quickly spread. Down south, in Kentucky, Virginia, the Carolinas and Georgia, they heard about the shining city in the heart of Manhattan that blacks were claiming as their own. And, weary of share cropping poverty, Jim Crow railway cars and savage lynchings, they headed north. The great migration had begun.

By 1920, black Harlem had become a reality, and its night life a legend. As early as 1913, New Yorkers had begun making the trip uptown in search of lively entertainment. Florenz Ziegfeld had seen a show called *Darktown Follies* at the Lafayette Theatre, and had raided it for contributions to his own Follies at 54th Street.

What turned those midnight excursions to Harlem from trickle to flood, was the advent, in 1920, of Prohibition. Whereas the downtown speakeasies were mostly dimly lit cellars where drinks were served in tea cups, and police raids were a regular event – up in Harlem, along the streets off Lenox Avenue, there were a hundred places where you could drink the night away, and with only an infrequent and half-hearted visit from the cops to interrupt the flow of liquor, which, rot gut though it was, had 'the kick of a Georgia mule'.

These clubs ranged all the way from the dives of 133rd Street, known as 'the Jungle' – Pod's and Jerry's, Banks,

Basement Brownie's and The Bucket Of Blood – to Happy Rhone's further uptown at 143rd Street, which was credited with being the first real Harlem night club, with uniformed waitresses and a floor show.

While a few of these clubs, like the Lenox Club (which was owned by blacks), did not welcome white customers, most of them, like Small's Paradise and the clubs in 'the Jungle', strove for a mixed clientèle. The biggest and the best of them, like the Cotton Club and Connie's Inn, barred blacks altogether.

The Cotton Club, which Lady Mountbatten called 'the aristocrat of Harlem', was at Lenox Avenue and 142nd Street. One flight up, and originally designed as a ballroom, it was a huge room seating from four to five hundred people. It had previously been run by the ex-heavyweight boxing champion, Jack Johnson, as the Club Deluxe, and when that enterprise failed, had been bought by the notorious bootlegger, Owney Madden, as a place to dispose of his beer to well-heeled New Yorkers. When it opened in 1927, Duke Ellington enlarged his band to play there. Network radio had arrived by 1924, and Ellington and his band broadcast almost every night. The club became famous throughout America, and when Duke began recording with his 'Cotton Club Orchestra', it became equally well known in London, Paris and Amsterdam.

But the true glory of the Cotton Club was the floor show. Gaudy and frenetic, a veritable explosion of energy, the shows were produced by Lew Leslie, and written by Dorothy Fields and Jimmy McHugh, and later by Harold Arlen. The stars were Ethel Waters, Adelaide Hall and Bill (Bojangles) Robinson. The girls in the chorus were all chosen for the lightness of their skin; golden brown, 'high yaller' girls whose sinuous dancing was to set the style for the swing era soon to follow. Duke himself wrote of them: 'They had twelve dancing girls and eight show girls, and they were all beautiful chicks. They used to dress so well! On Sunday nights, when celebrities filled the joint, they would rush out of the dressing room after the show in all their finery. Every time they went by, the stars and the rich people would be saying, "My, who is *that*?" '

Connie's Inn, on Seventh Avenue, owned by the Immerman brothers, Connie and George, was the place that, in 1929, made Louis Armstrong a star. The revue *Hot Chocolates* had songs written by the young Fats Waller (he had once been a delivery boy in the Immermans' Harlem delicatessen), and his lyricist, Andy Razaf. Among the songs were 'Ain't Misbehavin'' and 'What Did I Do To Be So Black And Blue'. The show went on to Broadway and ran for two hundred and nineteen performances.

If the real Harlemites were turned away from the doors of the Cotton Club and Connie's Inn, they were not unduly concerned. Most of them could not afford the prices anyway. What they really wanted to do was dance, and the place to do that was the Savoy Ballroom. The Savoy was a marvel, and its opening night in 1926, pandemonium. The advance publicity promised: 'You will be bombarded with a barrage of the most electrifying spasms of entertainment ever assembled under one roof', and for once the blurb writers didn't lie.

The building was huge, a block long. Four thousand people could dance to the music of two bands. You entered through a spacious lobby and mounted a marble staircase beneath a cut-glass chandelier. The dance hall was decorated in orange and blue; there was a soda fountain and tables set upon deep pile carpet. Moe Gale, the proprietor, had spent more than two hundred thousand dollars on it. Harlem took the Savoy to its heart, and 'Stompin' At The Savoy' became a way of life. Romare Bearden, a black artist, used to go there three times a week (admission cost fifty cents, Sundays and holidays, seventy-five cents) because 'the best dancing in the world was there, and the best music'.

When the stock market collapsed in 1929, the bands played on, scarcely missing a beat. *Variety*, the show business bible, noted: 'Night life [in Harlem] now surpasses that of Broadway itself. From midnight until after dawn it is a seething cauldron of Nubian mirth and hilarity.' But if thriving night clubs, theatres and ballrooms were evidence that the Depression had simply passed Harlem by, it was illusory. Like many another metropolis, there were two Harlems living side by side, one scarcely aware of the existence of the other. As the comedian Jimmy Durante wrote in 1931, in a book about night clubs: 'The average coloured man you see along the streets in Harlem, doesn't know any more about these dumps than the old maid in North Forks, South Dakota.'

In fact, for workaday Harlem, times were bitterly hard. The *New York Herald Tribune* reported: 'The Depression caused five times as much unemployment in Harlem as in any other part of the city.' In 1931 there were 200,000 people in Harlem, and half of them were on relief. Unemployment and high rents were turning Harlem into a slum; for the first time, people were beginning to refer to it as a ghetto.

Overcrowding was acute. Two and three families were living in apartments intended for one; some boarding-houses rented beds by the day, the night, even by the hour. Many people were going hungry. Night clubs and theatres organised concerts for charity. On Christmas Eve 1934, Owney Madden, the gangster who ran the Cotton Club, handed out three thousand food parcels each containing a five pound chicken and assorted fruit and vegetables.

Rent parties, those impromptu gatherings where the guests bring food and drink, and subscribe to their host's expenses, always an important feature of Harlem life, now became a dire necessity. In 1931, evictions for non-payment of rent were running at about twenty a day.

In 1933, the worst year of the Depression, the Brotherhood of Sleeping Car Porters was thrown out of its headquarters building on 136th Street. Benjamin McLaurin, one of the union organisers, found an apartment on 140th Street: 'I promoted a weekly rent party, to get money to pay rent. It was the only income we had ... Saturday mornings I spent preparing food and most of the day cooking. I cooked chitterlings and pigs' feet ... I cooked

8

so much of that stuff that it nauseates me now. I don't want to be around if anybody is cooking it.'

Red Saunders, a drummer from Memphis, gave Studs Terkel his description of rent parties in *Hard Times*: 'They were black speakeasies ... houses where people lived, with a piano in the front room where people danced. And moonshine, twenty-five cents a half-pint. Pulverised alcohol, no admission. The money came from the sale of moonshine and supper. Spaghetti and chili ... the house'd be packed all kinds of way. Six, five, sometimes four rooms, a hundred and eighty people would be in it.'

'A room full of dancing couples, scarcely moving their feet, arms completely encircling one another's bodies' wrote the novelist Wallace Thurman. 'Cheeks being warmed by one another's breath ... eyes closed ... animal ecstasy agitating their perspiring faces. There was much panting, much hip movement, much shaking of the buttocks....'

This, then, was the Harlem that the girl from Yonkers saw and heard, and dreamed of conquering.

Ella Fitzgerald was born on April 25th, 1918, in Newport News, Virginia. Virginia is the most northerly of the southern United States, and Newport News, at the mouth of the James River, is a major port for transatlantic and coastal shipping. It is also one of the world's largest ship-building and repair centres: America's first nuclear-powered aircraft carrier, the U.S.S. *Enterprise*, was built there.

Ella scarcely remembers her father. She was told that the house was always full of music, her mother singing in a sweet soprano voice, her father playing his guitar. When he died, shortly after the Great War, and life in Newport News became a desperate struggle for survival, mother and daughter joined the great migration and moved north. They settled in Yonkers, just across the Hudson River from the Bronx. In Yonkers, Mrs Fitzgerald had a sister. There they might find help and the possibility of an easier life.

Growing up in Yonkers (a mixed neighbourhood), Ella

made friends mostly with the Italian kids at her school. Faced with a choice of subjects ('You had to take art or music, and I knew I was no artist'), she learned to read music. Sadly, this early facility was soon lost, and she has always envied singers like Sarah Vaughan and Carmen McRae who can read music with such ease. For a while she took private piano lessons, but the five dollars that they cost was more than her mother could afford, and she soon had to give them up.

Like many of her schoolfriends, she did what she could to help the family finances. 'To make extra money, I used to take numbers,' she remembers. The numbers game was the illegal, gangster-run lottery which was the New Yorker's favourite form of gambling in those days. And she acted as lookout for the local whorehouse. She'd watch the street and knock on the door to let the girls know when the cops were on the prowl. 'Oh yes,' she says, 'I had a very interesting young life.'

And there was music everywhere. The radio and the gramophone brought the exciting sounds of Harlem (that shining black city only a few miles away) right into her room. By 1927, there were two radio networks, and Duke Ellington and his famous orchestra had begun broadcasting from the Cotton Club. As for gramophone records, it is often said that the golden age of jazz recordings was the period between 1926 and 1929. Besides Ellington, there were Louis Armstrong, Luis Russell, Fletcher Henderson, Jimmy Lunceford, and the white musicians who had mastered the form: Benny Goodman, Jack Teagarden, the Dorsey Brothers, Red Nichols and Miff Mole.

As for singers, as early as 1920, Okeh records had released 'You Can't Keep A Good Man Down', sung by Mamie Smith, the first recording by a black vocalist. And the following year, the Black Swan label ('The Only Genuine Coloured Record – Others Are Only Passing for Coloured') issued the first recordings by Ethel Waters, 'Down Home Blues', with 'Oh Daddy' on the flip side.

Certainly, her earliest musical enthusiasms had little to

10

do with jazz. One of her first heroes was an enormously popular singer, a regular cornball, named Arthur Tracy, who billed himself as 'The Street Singer'. He had his own radio show on CBS, and sang songs like 'The Wheel Of The Waggon Is Broken', and 'Marta (Rambling Rose of the Wildwood)', in a lachrymose, vibrato-laden voice. In later years, her musician friends would howl with laughter whenever she revealed such juvenile tastes.

At Junior High School she belonged to the Glee Club. She enjoyed the company of her friends, but the singing didn't interest her all that much. She got into a school play and sang 'Sing You Sinners', yet another of those Tin Pan Alley demeaning stereotypes of negro life.

> You sinners, drop ev'rything,
> Let that harmony ring,
> Up to heaven and sing,
> Sing you sinners!

Her friends thought she was so good, she ought to think about doing it for a living. Ella had dreams about being a Broadway star like Ethel Waters, who that year was wowing 'em in *As Thousands Cheer* with Irving Berlin's 'Heat Wave'.

But her shyness almost defeated her. Faced by an audience that was not made up of people she knew, she would freeze.

Out of childhood and into her teens, she soon became aware of Harlem at first hand – how could she not? It was only just down the road apiece – and Harlem was where, in today's parlance, it surely was at.

She was always a child of the Harlem streets; hanging around with her friends on Seventh Avenue corners, waylaying celebrities, begging autographs. She remembers getting Chick Webb's: 'It was winter – and his hands were freezing cold, but he signed that autograph for me.' And shyly asking Billie Holiday for hers. Billie Holiday, only three years older than Ella, but already, in 1933, singing in night clubs and recording with Benny Goodman.

So how long before the girl from the Yonkers would

savour the true essence? How long before she would scrape together her fifty cents and dance at the holy of holies, the Savoy?

Because dance was what she most seriously and passionately wanted to do. Who didn't? New York was dance crazy in those days. And Harlem crazier than anywhere else. Years before, in 1914, Adam Clayton Powell Senior, one of the moral leaders of a growing black community, had sounded a note of apocalyptic disapproval: 'The Negro race is dancing itself to death.' It was ragtime then – the Turkey Trot, the Bunny Hug, the Texas Tommy (the great Scott Joplin himself had settled in Harlem in 1915); but came the jazz age, and Adam Clayton Powell's harsh prophecy looked as if it might indeed come true. The Lindy Hop, that dance in which the girl whirls away from her partner and only his restraining hand will prevent her spinning off into the void, was invented in Harlem in the late twenties, and the Savoy Ballroom was its home, its very fountain-head.

'I always wanted to be a dancer,' says Ella. She tried to imitate the one and only Earl 'Snakehips' Tucker, the eccentric dancer who, in 1927, had caused a sensation in that year's Cotton Club Revue. Says Jim Haskins in his book about the Cotton Club: 'He could twist his haunches and thigh joints into unbelievable contortions.'

And Ella was a good dancer. 'In Yonkers I was known as one of their great little tap dancers.' And she remained mad about dancing for years to come. When, in 1940, she went on tour with Dizzy Gillespie, she and Dizzy 'used to do the Lindy Hop a lot. We would go into towns and go to clubs – there'd be a nightclub or somewhere to go, and that was it! We used to take the floor over. Yeah, do the Lindy Hop because we could do it. Yeah, we danced like mad together. Dizzy was a good dancer. Both of us were good dancers. And we'd go with all the old Savoy steps.'

Yeah. So naturally, when, at sixteen years of age, she had screwed up her courage to enter an amateur talent contest, she'd decided she was going to dance. And then, facing that sea of faces, that menacingly murmurous mob, her knees had started knocking, her nerve had failed her, and instead of dancing she had sung. 'That time, I didn't know one key from another. I just sang. They just played and I tried to sing in the key they picked for me.'

Winning first prize was the real spur. The money was truly a Godsend. She must have had some whiff of revelation that, if she was about to set out on the road to fame and fortune, this might very well be the route to take.

Every aspiring singer has a special favourite, somebody they begin by imitating, can fantasise about sounding like – and later, if they are ever going to be any good, somebody whose influence they will absorb and meld into their own individual style.

In 1934, most of the guys wanted to be Bing Crosby, eating the microphone and boo-boo-booing into their boots. Or, if they were hep to the jive, they were growling 'Yeah!' like Louis Armstrong, and howling 'Hi de hi!' like Cab Calloway.

If you were a girl, you could belt it like Ethel Merman, or croon it sweetly like Kate Smith. And, if you were into the blues, you could wail it like Bessie Smith or Ma Rainey. Ella herself would soon enough be the object of such sound-alike imitation. Looking back at 1938 when 'A-Tisket, A-Tasket' was the hit of the year, John Hammond, then a young record producer, complained: 'From coast to coast, young girls were copying Ella, sometimes note for note.'

Having grown out of her Arthur Tracy, the street singer, phase, Ella's favourite singer was Connee Boswell, a nice white girl from New Orleans, who was the lead singer with her sisters, Martha and Helvetia (Vet), in a close harmony act called the Boswell Sisters. This was the act which invented the singing style which was to set the scene for the Andrews Sisters, and for all the vocal trios, quartettes and quintettes, which sang with the big bands of the swing era, soon to follow.

The Boswell sisters were all classically trained; they had played with the New Orleans Philharmonic Orchestra, and Connee had mastered not only the cello and the piano, but also the saxophone. It showed in her orchestrations for the act, which echoed the section writing being used by arrangers like Fletcher Henderson and Don Redman. It is perhaps noteworthy that the trio's signature tune, 'Shout, Sister, Shout' had been written at the turn of the century by a black composer named Tim Brymn, who had led, in 1915, a twenty-piece band at the New York Roof Garden. A true pioneer of jazz.

Connee Boswell was a good model. Ella's bold clarity of delivery, her precise, musicianly intonation, which seems to have changed little over the years, is clearly influenced by Connee and her singing sisters.

And so, Ella launched herself on to the Amateur Night circuit. There were plenty to choose from: besides the Harlem Opera House, there was the Lafayette Theatre at Seventh Avenue and 132nd Street. The Lafayette was known as the cradle of stars, and it attracted an audience more merciless to amateurs than any other in Harlem. The following year, the theatre was taken over by the Federal Theatre Project, a part of President Roosevelt's New Deal for subsidizing the arts. It was there that John Houseman presented a black *Hamlet*, directed by the young and extravagantly talented Orson Welles.

Ella's repertoire still consisted of just three songs: 'Believe It, Beloved', 'The Object Of My Affection' and 'Judy'. These she sang on every Amateur Night in Harlem. On one occasion, greatly daring, she decided to try something new. It was a Dorothy Fields and Frank McHugh song called 'Lost In A Fog'. She didn't know it well, and the pianist who accompanied her ('You just start, honey, I'll follow you') knew it not at all. Halfway through the chorus, Ella stumbled over a phrase, paused, tried to start again, and with absolutely no help from the pianist, finally had to give it up. The audience, with their customary grace and charity, did what was expected of them. Says Ella: 'They booed me off the stage.' It was to be the first and only time such a dreadful thing would happen. Ella ran home in tears. Her mother comforted her as best she could. 'Keep trying, child. Keep trying.'

And Ella kept trying. In February 1935, she once again entered the competition at the Harlem Opera House. She won again – the first prize, a week's work starting the following Friday, singing with the star attraction, Tiny Bradshaw and his band. Myron 'Tiny' Bradshaw was a singer who had worked with the Mills Blue Rhythm Band and with Luis Russell. A few months earlier he had formed his own band to play at the Renaissance Ballroom and to do some recording with American Decca.

But Ella had a problem; she had simply nothing to wear that was suitable for such an occasion. Her clothes were all hand-me-downs and cast-offs – she didn't even own a decent pair of shoes. Tiny Bradshaw, the boys in his band and the girls in the chorus all chipped in to buy her a gown, and in her brand new finery she was ready to go to work.

They put her on right at the end of the show, when the audience were already donning their overcoats and preparing to face the bitter cold outside. Tiny Bradshaw urged them to stay. 'Ladies and gentlemen,' he announced. 'Here's the young girl that's been winning all the contests.' And, Ella remembers, 'They all came back and took off their coats and sat down again.'

And all over Harlem, people began to take notice of the gawky girl from Yonkers with a voice which was just like a bell.

Among them was Benny Carter, a brilliant young musician who had recently formed his own band. Carter spoke to his friend, John Hammond Junior, a well-born New Yorker, kinsman of Vanderbilts, who had decided to devote his life to the world of jazz, and in particular to advancing the cause of black musicians. Together, they took Ella to see Fletcher Henderson at his house on Striver's Row, that affluent section of Harlem at 138th and 139th Street, between Seventh and Eighth Avenues. Ella had never seen such splendour. Henderson was the leader of what Hammond considered 'the greatest band in the country'. Ella sang for him, but as she recalls: 'I guess I didn't make too much of an impression, because he said

15

he'd get in touch with me later, but nothing ever happened.'

Word had now reached the offices of the Columbia Broadcasting System, one of the two mighty radio networks, away downtown. An audition was arranged, and CBS offered her a guest appearance on the radio show hosted by none other than Arthur Tracy, the Street Singer! A contract was drawn up. It was the chance of her young lifetime.

'My mother signed the contract,' says Ella. 'And they were going to build me up as a discovery.' Sadly, it was not to be. Ella's mother died. That meant that there was now nobody legally qualified to sign documents on her behalf; the contract was no longer valid.

Ella went to live with an aunt, but that seems not to have satisfied the authorities either. Before long she was admitted to the Riverdale Orphanage in Yonkers.

At the orphanage, they concentrated on preparing their charges for life in the world outside. Ella was taught typewriting, and it is a mark of her nimble intelligence that she became expert. Years later, a Gale Agency publicity handout declared that she could 'still pound a mean typewriter. While addressing a graduating class of Buchanan Business Institute, Miss Fitzgerald entered a speed-writing competition. She didn't win, but was placed second, doing 290 words in the four-minute test.'

The institutional life she now led seems however to have been not all that restrictive. She continued to escape to Harlem, and to enter every amateur contest she could.

In 1934, Leo Brecher, the owner of the Lafayette, acquired Hurtig and Seamon's Music Hall, next door to the Harlem Opera House. As well as the Lafayette, he also owned the Olympia, the Plaza and the Little Carnegie theatres, and he ran them together with a local impresario named Frank Schiffman. Brecher and Schiffman renamed Hurtig and Seamon's the Apollo, and it was to become one of the most famous theatres in America.

Frank Schiffman was born on the lower East Side and educated at the City College of New York, where one of his classmates had been Edward G. Robinson. He knew and understood the people of Harlem, and spent most of his life managing theatres there. At the Lafayette he had presented such notable stars as Bessie Smith, the Mills Brothers, Ethel Waters and Bill Robinson; also the bands of Duke Ellington, Jimmy Lunceford, Fletcher Henderson and Earl Hines. It was his intention to continue that policy at the Apollo. He announced that it would be 'the finest theatre in Harlem'. The first presentation under the new ownership was to be a 'lavish and colourful' show featuring Ralph Cooper, Aida Ward and Benny Carter and his orchestra. It was announced also that a regular part of the stage show would be an amateur contest for young singers, and that the winner would be offered a week's work with whatever band was playing.

The audience at the Lafayette was noted for its merciless treatment of amateur talent it disapproved of. It soon became apparent that the Apollo was bent on matching that reputation, and, if possible, enhancing it. Nancy Cunard, an upper-class Englishwoman who loved Harlem night life, wrote in her book *Negro*, that Apollo theatregoers would reject untried talent of a sort that 'would have passed with honour anywhere out of America.' In short, it was clearly understood that no popular entertainer could be said to have arrived until he or she had faced that sixteen hundred capacity audience and won its approval.

Frank Schiffman's son Bobby is quoted by Ted Fox in his book *Showtime at the Apollo*: 'When performers hit the Apollo stage, no matter how celebrated they were, they were nervous ... Every performer was, but it keyed them up. It spurred them on to do the best they possibly could. They did their best at the Apollo because they knew that if they sang it wrong or didn't give their all, the audience would jump right at them.'

The Apollo was also a movie house, and the stage show, which came between the films, went on five times a day, thirty-one times a week. Wednesday night was Amateur Night, and Frank Schiffman and his two sons, Bobby and Jack, having auditioned dozens of acts in the basement

17

rehearsal room, would then choose six of them for the ten o'clock show. Such was the lure of Apollo Amateur Nights that some of those young hopefuls might have to wait for weeks before they were given the chance to get up there and do their stuff. Winners were decided by acclamation. The M.C. would hold his hand over the head of each of the contestants, and the audience would applaud. The lucky ones were given a week's work (the week started on Friday at the Apollo), and a prize of fifty dollars. Through the years the honours list of winners became truly impressive. There was Bill Kenny, lead singer with the Ink Spots, Sarah Vaughan, Pearl Bailey, Leslie Uggams, James Brown, Wilson Pickett, Dionne Warwick and Gladys Knight.

The losers, however, suffered a miserable fate. It was a time-honoured tradition at the Apollo, that should one of the contestants fail to please, a stage hand named Norman Miller (but known to one and all as Porto Rico) would rush out wearing a weird and wonderful costume of his own devising, and, firing a cap pistol, chase the poor amateur right off the stage. The audience enjoyed this cruel ritual so much, that should there be among the night's contestants no obvious candidate for the Porto Rico treatment, the stage hands would fake it, by hauling some innocent off the street to be the sacrificial lamb.

And then one night it was Ella Fitzgerald's turn to face the hanging jury at the Apollo. She walked out on to the stage, knees knocking as usual. She sang her three songs and won first prize: a week's work and fifty dollars.

Among the appreciative audience that week at the Apollo was one Bardu Ali, a handsome, well-dressed young man, who worked at the Savoy Ballroom, a little further uptown. Bardu often dropped in at the Apollo, in search of a little relaxation, and perhaps a few laughs. But this time, there was this skinny kid up there on the stage, and she really could sing up a storm.

She sang 'The Object Of My Affection', and although you could hear the influence of Connee Boswell, she also had something of her own. And the voice was remarkable. 'Hey, listen to that!' he said to himself. 'This chick sings just like a horn.'

Bardu Ali went to work that night at the Savoy, where he had an interesting job; he was the 'leader' of the Chick Webb band – that is to say, he stood in front of it, made the announcements, joked with the customers and generally made himself pleasant, while the real boss, Chick Webb himself, sat behind his drum kit and got on with the serious business of making music.

Chick Webb had been bringing his band to the Savoy on and off since 1927, and his was just about the most popular band that famous dance hall ever had. He was born in Baltimore, Maryland, in 1902, and arrived in New York in 1924. Crippled early in life by a tubercular spine, he became a drummer of quite awesome power.

He formed his first band in 1926, and Duke Ellington claims some credit for this. At the time, Ellington was leading a small band at a night club called the Kentucky, at Forty-ninth Street and Broadway. It was a place where other musicians would drop in after work. Remembering those nights, Ellington later wrote: 'When some of the boys around downtown decided to open up a new joint, they would stop by and tell Sonny Greer and me, "We need a band." We went uptown and hired five or six musicians, and Chick was one of them.

"Now, you're the bandleader," I said to Chick.

"Man, I don't want to be no bandleader," he answered.

"All you do is collect the money and bring me mine."

"Is that all I have to to?"

"Yeah."

"Okay, I'm the bandleader." '

The following year Chick took his band to play at the Savoy for the first time, and although they played the Roseland Ballroom off Times Square, the Cotton Club in Harlem, and toured around for a while, by the mid-thirties they had become the band the Savoy simply could not do without.

The bands which played at the Savoy were big and

powerful. They needed to be. In a hall which could pack in five thousand dancers, the beat was all important, the drummer the man who made it, and Chick Webb the drummer who made it best of all. Sam Woodyard, who played drums with Duke Ellington in the fifties, said this of Chick Webb: 'He was the first drummer who made sense in a big band . . . He knew how to shade and colour, and how to bring a band up and keep it there.'

Other drummers, white as well as black, came to the Savoy to listen and to learn. Buddy Rich, the drummer with Artie Shaw and Tommy Dorsey, and later a big band leader in his own right, when interviewed by Whitney Balliet of the *New Yorker* in 1972, said: 'Chick Webb was startling. He was a tiny man with this big face and big, stiff shoulders. He sat up on a kind of throne and used a twenty-eight inch bass drum which had special pedals for his feet and he had those old-goose-neck cymbal-holders. Every beat was like a bell.' And Gene Krupa, demon drummer in the great days of the Benny Goodman band, recalled: 'That man was dynamic; he could reach the most amazing heights. When he really let go, you had the feeling that the entire atmosphere was being charged.'

Seated on his 'throne' in the middle of his band, and therefore somewhat remote from the dancers, he must have felt the need for a 'front man', and that was why he employed Bardu Ali to stand up there and do his nodding and smiling for him. That night, Bardu mentioned that he'd heard a girl singing at the Apollo, who had the makings, but Chick didn't want to know.

It should be noted here, that singers in bands, vocalists, they were called then, and especially girl vocalists, were not highly thought of by the bands of that time. A jazz magazine called *Swing* noted: 'Ask any ten bandleaders as to their pet headache . . . nine will answer "girl vocalists". . . . Yes, girl vocalists are a nuisance.' And *Down Beat* observed that 'chirpers' are 'always looked down on by musicians as unhip dress extras.'

Jazz is a language, shared in common by all the musicians

who were inaugurating the new swing era. Duke Ellington had already written the music whose text would serve as its motto: 'It Don't Mean A Thing If It Ain't Got That Swing.' It is easier to describe what swing isn't than to describe what it is. What it isn't is the music played for dancing in the plush New York hotels, by bands like Guy Lombardo's, or in London by Bert Ambrose. Swing speaks the language of jazz; it engages the creative energies of all who play it. It is vital, urgent, infinitely expressive. Singers were 'unhip'. They didn't speak the language; they didn't swing. Singers were not only a nuisance, they were also a powerful irritant. Singers who anticipated the beat, or used the despised short quaver, a leftover from ragtime days, could drive musicians wild. And poor intonation, the inability to sing in tune, a common enough failing even among the most popular singers of the day, was a crime worthy of instant ex-communication.

So Chick Webb's response to Bardu Ali's enthusiastic report on Ella was not encouraging. He already had a singer with his band. His name was Charlie Linton, and Dizzy Gillespie remembers him as a 'suave dark guy' who sang in a high voice 'like Orlando Roberson'. And anyway, he simply wasn't interested in girl singers. Webb's reputation at the Savoy was based squarely on the fact that his was a great band to dance to. Ellington later wrote: 'Chick Webb was a dance-drummer who painted pictures of dances with his drums. The reason he had such control, such command of his audiences at the Savoy ballroom, was because he was always in communication with the dancers and felt it the way they did.' So what use were girl singers to him? Who needs 'em?

A few days later, Chick Webb and the band arrived at the Apollo to start a week's engagement. One evening, Bardu Ali strolled on to the stage between shows, and there was Ella: 'She was standing in the wings, with some boys' shoes on, eating a hot dog.' Bardu told her that he'd heard her sing, had liked what he'd heard, and had told his boss, Chick Webb about her.

'Does he want to hear me sing?' asked Ella.

'I don't know. But now's a good time to find out.' Bardu took Ella's hand, and together they mounted the stairs to Chick's dressing room.

'Chick,' said Bardu. 'This is the girl I told you about. I would like very much for you to hear her sing.'

Chick, who was dozing in an armchair, opened one eye and looked at the gawky schoolgirl in the boys' shoes. 'You're kidding,' he said. He had a gruff bass voice which sounded more intimidating than it really was.

'I'm not kidding,' said Bardu. 'Trust me. This is the greatest voice in the world.'

So Ella sang a few bars of 'The Object Of My Affection'. The room was full of noisy musicians, but as Bardu tells it: 'You could hear a pin drop.'

Chick listened. Ella sang unaccompanied, but the pitch was perfect. In the Chick Webb band they would marvel at it: 'You could tune your instrument to it.'

Chick was impressed. He felt he ought to do something about it. But like most bandleaders of the time, he didn't make the final decisions. He picked up the phone and called the man who did.

Besides being the owner of the Savoy Ballroom, Moe Gale was also Chick Webb's manager. With his brother Tim, he ran the Gale Agency, an organization which specialized in representing black bands and black entertainers. Much has been written about the exploitative nature of the white manager/black band relationship – Joe Glaser and Louis Armstrong, Irving Mills and Duke Ellington – but that is the way things were; the manager set the deals, paid the band as little as the traffic would allow, and pocketed the rest.

Moe Gale came to the theatre, and Chick produced Ella. 'You're kidding,' said Moe Gale.

'Don't look at her,' said Chick. 'Just listen to the voice.'

Ella sang. Moe listened. 'So what do you want to do?' said Moe.

'Well,' said Chick. 'We've got this gig tomorrow night.

The fraternity dance. I'd like to take the kid with me. Try her out with the band.'

'And who's gonna pay her?' demanded Moe. 'Because I ain't.'

It was well known to Chick and even to his musicians, that managers were paid thousands of dollars for these college dates, but paid out only a fraction of it to the bandleader and his men, but let that pass.

'I will,' said Chick. 'I'll pay her out of my own pocket.'

That may sound unusual behaviour on the part of a bandleader, but trombonist Dicky Wells, in his book *The Night People*, assures us that if he thought it would help his band, no sacrifice was too great. 'Chick went hungry a lot just to keep the band in music. He would live on hamburgers so he could buy arrangements.'

'The next day,' Ella remembers, 'I got on the band bus for New Haven. It was like going into another world.'

New Haven is but an hour's drive from New York City, but the dance they were on their way to play at was at Yale University, America's most venerable Ivy League campus. There they were, those scrubbed and crew-cut college boys in their Brooks Brothers suits and their buttoned-down shirts; those pretty bright-eyed co-eds – all out there on the dance floor, Lindy-hopping to the wild and reckless Harlem music of Chick Webb and his band. Another world indeed.

Ella sang her three songs, and the college kids hung around the bandstand yelling for more. Bardu Ali remembers it well: 'The kids were all saying, "We want to hear the girl sing."'

Chick Webb was almost convinced. The girl was something special. He had found a treasure. On the bus back home, he talked quietly to her. How would she like to sing with his band at the Savoy? Just for a week. A try out. How would she like it? Her knees began to knock. Yes, she would like it very much. She surely would. You bet. And thank you, thank you very much, Mr Webb.

At the age of seventeen, Ella Fitzgerald was about to become a fully fledged professional singer.

Fletcher Henderson was the man most responsible for the shape and substance of the big band sound which from the early 30s was to set the scene for a decade or more of swing music. Known to his fellow musicians as 'Smack', he was born in Georgia in 1898, the son of cultivated, middle-class parents. He graduated from Atlanta University in 1920, and in the summer of that year he enrolled at Columbia University in New York to study for a master's degree in chemistry. Finding that his money would not last until the autumn term began, he took various jobs as a pianist, as song demonstrator for a music publisher, and as accompanist to the singer, Ethel Waters. In 1923 he became the leader of a band at the Club Alabam; two years later he moved to the Roseland Ballroom on Broadway, and stayed there for five years.

The Roseland was a great barn of a place, and a band had to blow some to fill it. To achieve this end, the band grew larger; by 1927 there were twelve men: five brass – three trumpets and two trombones; three saxophones – two altos and a tenor; and a rhythm section of four – piano, tuba, drums and banjo. In order that such a large band should play together, it was necessary that the music be written down and that the musicians be able to read it. And so there emerged a most important figure in the history of popular dance music: the arranger.

In Henderson's case, the arranger was Don Redman, an immensely talented musician – a child prodigy who had played the trumpet at the age of three, and had completed his musical studies at Boston and Detroit Conservatories. Redman it was who refined the antiphonal character of big

24

band music (probably drawing inspiration from Negro church music), and the call-and-response interplay between the front line sections of the band, the reeds and the brass. This, in its turn, led to the emergence of the two most important and valued members of the band, the leaders of those two sections; the first trumpet and the first alto saxophone. They were the men who carried the melody and dictated the phrasing for the other members of their sections to follow. It was Redman himself, along with Benny Carter and Johnny Hodges (of the Duke Ellington orchestra), who supplied the template for all other lead alto players to copy.

By 1933, when the banjo and tuba in the rhythm section had been replaced by the more nimble guitar and string bass, and Henderson had added a second tenor to his saxophone section, the swing band had taken on its definitive form.

In that year, Prohibition ended, and although there were gloomy predictions that legal liquor would mean the end of white interest in Harlem, it didn't actually happen. Not yet anyway (after the race riot of 1935, whites became noticeably less keen to visit their favourite uptown night clubs, and the even bigger riot of 1943 was to turn Harlem into a virtual no-go area).

The Depression was biting hard. And while white musicians, especially those interested in playing jazz, were finding it difficult to get work, the black musicians, albeit at cut-rate wages, were thriving. Their way of playing dance music was beginning to take hold. In 1933 Duke Ellington left the Cotton Club to visit England with his 'Famous Orchestra', following Louis Armstrong who had headlined at the London Palladium the previous year. Jimmy Lunceford, Luis Russell, Cab Calloway and Don Redman all had big bands, and Count Basie was waiting in the wings.

And Chick Webb was at the Savoy.

Charles Buchanan was manager at the Savoy, and he ran a tight ship. In an interview he gave Jervis Anderson of the

New Yorker, he said: 'A key to the success of the Savoy was that we maintained such a standard of order that girls were not afraid to come. We had burly fellows, dressed in tuxedos, who threw any trouble maker out.'

There were two bands, and the work was hard. Taft Jordan, distinguished trumpet player and veteran of the Chick Webb band, remembers: 'We'd open at 7.30 p.m. The first band played from 7.30 to 9.30. The next band came on and played from 9.30 to 10.30. Then alternate every hour. [On Saturday night] from 7.30 until 6 o'clock Sunday morning.'

All the same, musicians loved working at the Savoy. The audience really appreciated a good band, and only the best could succeed there and be invited back. The best of them had all worked there: Jimmy Lunceford, Duke Ellington, Benny Moten, Earl Hines, Claude Hopkins and Fletcher Henderson. Later the white bands, with much trepidation, ventured in, daring to compete with the black bands they had admired for so long: Benny Goodman, Tommy Dorsey and Charlie Barnet all played there at least once.

It would be wrong to think that power-house swing was the only kind of music which would satisfy this choosy audience. Taft Jordan again: 'We played everything that people danced to. We played waltzes. We played Latin numbers.' It is said that the band that pulled in the biggest crowd in the history of the Savoy, was the sweetest of all sweet bands, Guy Lombardo and his Royal Canadians!

Be that as it may, it was out and out swing which was the meat in the sandwich. Says Charlie Buchanan: 'The best band is the one that keeps the floor filled.' And Dickie Wells, trombonist with both Fletcher Henderson and Count Basie, adds: 'If you didn't swing, you weren't there for long.'

'Half the bands that developed in the twenties and thirties did so because of the Savoy,' said Charlie Buchanan. 'They had a place to start, a place to perfect their arrangements. I would hire them for a couple of weeks and then Frank Schiffman at the Lafayette and later at the Apollo

26

would take them. In this way we kept them working. As long as you kept them working, the better they became.'

Chick Webb's band was the best. By 1935, he was by common consent 'King of the Savoy'.

Charlie Buchanan remembers the night Chick Webb brought Ella Fitzgerald to the ballroom. She was 'young, simple, an orphan. We had no money, but we had the budget. So I said to Chick, "I'll put ten dollars, and you put ten dollars." We pooled the twenty dollars and hired Ella. The second week we payed her fifty dollars. The third week we dressed her up.'

Chick was very protective of this young, simple girl. Almost immediately the question of Ella's legal status arose. New York City laws were stringent in the matter of the employment of minors – as Ella had already discovered after her mother's death had scotched her chances of a radio contract. Without somebody willing to be responsible for her welfare, she would have to stay at the orphanage. Chick talked the problem through with his wife. They agreed: the only way for little orphan Ella to turn professional was for the Webbs to adopt her – to become her legal guardians.

The papers were signed. Ella left the orphanage, and moved in with the Webbs. For the first time in her life, she had a mother *and* a father.

Chick Webb was in no hurry to foist his 'treasure' on the public. 'Slowly,' he would say. 'Slowly. There's lots to learn. Slowly.' Ella remembers: 'He used to tell me, you never want to be someone who goes up fast, because you come down the same way. And you meet the same people coming down as you do going up.'

He taught her how to sing with a big band. 'Listen to the beat, child. Relax, you're rushing it. Go with the beat. Always *with* the beat. That's it. Yeah! Now you're swinging.' She needed no lessons in singing. The voice was always there. A marvellous instrument. And, as time would tell, virtually indestructible. As to the way she looked, well, let's face it, that was something else. Said Moe Gale, 'She looked incredible – her hair dishevelled, her clothes just terrible.' Chick replied, 'Mr Gale, you'd be surprised what a beauty parlour and some make-up and nice clothes can do.' The boys in the band kidded her. They all called her 'Sis'. It was, 'Hey Sis, what's with the hairdo?' Ella just grinned, and took it all in good part.

After some months, and when he thought she was ready, Chick would allow her to sit on the bandstand for one or two of the sets, and sing a couple of choruses. He taught her bandstand deportment: how to stand at the microphone, what to do with those awkward hands. She learned fast, discovering a kind of simple repose. Chick was proud of his protégée.

Peter Dean, who became a professional singer and cabaret artist, was a schoolboy in 1935: 'I formed a club out of the George Washington High School band. We went to the Savoy Ballroom every Friday night and caught all those wonderful bands. We frequented the Savoy so much that we got to know that fabulous Chick Webb rather well. One night he slid up to me and said, "Hey, Peter, I want you to meet a little girl, and I want you to hear this girl sing." And he trotted out a very frightened and nervous youngster wearing a gingham dress and with a flower in her hair. She was so young and beautiful that we all fell in love with her before she opened her mouth. I can't recall the song she sang, but after the first chorus, the response was electric and all her nervousness faded away. We were all captivated.'

Mary Lou Williams was the gifted pianist and arranger with Andy Kirk and his Twelve Clouds of Joy, who worked mainly in Kansas City. Visiting New York, she found herself dancing at the Savoy: 'I heard a voice that sent chills up my spine ... I almost ran to the bandstand to find out who belonged to the voice, and saw a pleasant-looking, brown-skinned girl, standing modestly and singing the greatest.'

Having recovered from the initial shock of finding a woman on their bandstand, the Chick Webb musicians soon got to like Ella. She was such a nice girl, always smiling,

28

always happy. Under Chick's eagle eye, they treated her with respect. Jazz musicians are a witty and profane lot, and the presence of a lady within earshot of their fruitier utterances can be awkward and inhibiting. Chick instructed them – watch your language, okay? When, in the 40s, Ella toured with Dizzy Gillespie, Dizzy said that Ella 'always played the role of a lady' – whereas, on the other hand, 'Sarah Vaughan acted just like one of the boys. She used the same language I used with the guys.'

Ella sat among the guys, and sang an occasional chorus. She would watch the dancers, the famous Savoy Lindy-hoppers, and often the temptation to join them would be too strong to resist. 'And between songs,' says Ella, 'when I wasn't singing, instead of being on the bandstand, I'd be out on the floor, dancing.'

Saturday night was when the Lindy-hoppers really came into their own – dance contest time. Leonard Feather, a wide-eyed young Englishman, seeing it all for the first time, wrote about it in *Melody Maker*, scarcely able to contain his excitement: 'Lindy-hopping is no formalized dance. Superficially it is an Apache dance in rhythm, with wide-sweeping, breathless movements that take the dancers into a world of their own and transform the audience into a shouting, foot-stamping mob of enraptured revellers. Occasionally a white or mixed couple will make a bid for the evening's honours. Usually there are about a dozen couples altogether, each of which in turn is called up to the bandstand and asked to select a number to accompany the dance.

'Nine out of ten are too excited to give the matter any consideration, and the first item which naturally enters their heads is Chick Webb's signature tune, "Get Together". The dance lasts for about two choruses, or until the couple have gone through their paces to everyone's satisfaction. All the dancers are amateurs; yet, among these shop-assistants, janitors, secretaries, out for their Saturday night fun, even the weakest pair could outdance most of the professional acts seen on the English stage.'

To the dancers, the Savoy was life itself. 'That's all they

had,' said Charlie Buchanan. 'We used to see the same kids come there every day. Some of them had holes in their shoes. But if you took pity on one of them and bought him a new pair of shoes, all of a sudden he couldn't dance. He wasn't accustomed to good shoes.'

The dancers loved Chick Webb. But what Chick really enjoyed was a battle. With one or another of the visiting bands. 'Webb was always battle-mad,' said Duke Ellington. 'And those guys used to take on every band that came up to play there.'

There was a legendary encounter in July of 1934 with Fletcher Henderson's band, when Chick and Smack fought it out for seven successive nights. 'And he'd rather they came on Fridays, Saturdays or Sundays,' said Dicky Wells, who sat on the other bandstand with Teddy Hill's band. 'Because then the place would be packed with dancers ... Chick used to sit back looking out the window while his band played early in the evening, but when the visiting band would get rough – here he would come, and that was it!'

Mary Lou Williams adds: 'Chick would wait until the opposition had blown its hottest numbers and then – during a so-so set – would unexpectedly bring his band fresh to the stand and wham into a fine arrangement, like Benny Carter's "Liza", that was hard to beat.'

Most famous battle of all, and the one which is enshrined forever in jazz folklore, was the one between Chick Webb's band and Benny Goodman's in May 1937. It was, according to *Age*, the Harlem newspaper, 'the first time that Harlem would get an opportunity to see the Goodman aggregation which included two Negroes (Teddy Wilson and Lionel Hampton) as featured musicians in action.' There were five thousand dancers in the ballroom, and another five thousand outside, fighting the cops to get near enough to hear the music.

The battle raged for five hours. Ella sang against the Benny Goodman Quartette. *Melody Maker* breathlessly reported: 'Ella Fitzgerald, in Joan of Arc fashion, thrust her cantations (sic!) against the Quartet using "Big Boy Blue" and "You Showed Me The Way" as her weapons, while the instrumental foursome came back with "I Got Rhythm" and "The Blues". The patrons just stood up and listened. No one danced.' Charters and Kundstadt, the jazz historians, recorded: 'The Goodman band played at their best, but they couldn't win the crowd away from little Chick. He finished the session with a drum solo winning a thunderous ovation, while Goodman and his drummer, Gene Krupa, just stood there shaking their heads.'

Away from such heady excitements, there was Chick Webb's daytime recording, an important part of the band's work, if only because it was a way of earning a little extra money.

The Chick Webb band's recording career had begun some years earlier with a couple of sides for Brunswick released under the name of The Jungle Band. These titles, a twelve bar blues called 'Jungle Mama', and another, 'Dog Bottom', have caused some confusion among record collectors, since The Jungle Band was a pseudonym allotted to Duke Ellington and his orchestra before Duke's burgeoning career had persuaded Brunswick to issue his records under his real name. Another Chick Webb session in 1931 is memorable for the presence of Benny Carter, who in that year spent three months with the band. In 1933, the band was chosen to back Louis Armstrong. This produced some sides on Victor, including 'That's My Home' and 'I Hate to Leave You Now'.

Records at that time were 78 r.p.m. two-sided ten-inch discs (twelve-inch discs were exclusively the domain of classical artists and orchestras), and played for an average of three minutes a side.

Edgar Sampson, who played alto saxophone with both Ellington and Fletcher Henderson, joined Chick Webb in 1933, and began composing some of the best instrumental numbers of the time, among them 'If Dreams Come True', 'Lullaby In Rhythm', 'Don't Be That Way', and the tune which seemed to express the spirit of those times to perfection: 'Stomping At The Savoy'. In 1934, they were all

31

recorded for Columbia and Chick Webb's fame began to spread.

But these were hard times, and in the summer of that year, Jack Kapp, who was head of Brunswick, decided that records were over-priced at seventy-five cents, and that what was needed was a line featuring popular artists which would sell at thirty-five cents. He was financed by Edward Lewis, who had created English Decca in 1931, and now wanted access to American names. Together they launched the American Decca Company, with studios on West 54th Street in New York.

Jack Kapp made no bones about his aims – he wanted his records to be cheap to make, and quick to sell, and to hell with artistic standards. John Hammond remembers the first products he released. They were 'among the worst ever pressed by an American recording company'.

The records may have been bad, but the timing was good. The first months of American Decca coincided with the astonishing rise of the machine which was to become the world's favourite way of enjoying popular music – the juke box.

Since 1919, when station KDKA, Pittsburgh, had begun regular scheduled broadcasting, the phonograph had started to go into a decline. By 1923 it was clear that the quality of sound reproduction on the radio was far superior to the tinny, scratchy noise the phonograph was capable of. In that year, the Radio Corporation of America made twenty million dollars on the sale of receiver sets.

Even the introduction of electrical recording in 1925 didn't help much. Radio was gaining ground year by year. In 1929, RCA sold 3,750,000 radio sets, and following the Wall Street crash in November, record sales slumped by ninety-four per cent. By 1932, the broadcasters were convinced that the phonograph (or the gramophone, depending on which side of the Atlantic you resided) had been sunk with all hands.

There was however, one survivor of the carnage – jazz. The radio networks, possibly aware of the awesome responsibilities of public broadcasting, were confining their musical offerings to light music; string orchestras playing selections from Viennese operetta – what somebody has called 'potted palm music'. Radio stations which featured jazz were severely criticized for fouling the air waves. John Krivine, in his history of the juke box, says: 'Because radio neglected this area of music, jazz records were the only category that survived the catastrophic drop in sales in 1930.' It is said that Bessie Smith kept Columbia afloat at this time, and likewise Victor and Brunswick began to emphasize their 'race' products.

The words 'juke box' derive from the juke joints, the shanty bars and cafes in the South, where Negroes entertained themselves. In the spring of 1928, a man named Homer E. Capehart ('I was the Daddy of them all') started to manufacture a machine he called the 'Orchestrope'. It was the first automatic record player that could play both sides of a stack of twenty-eight records.

Among the first to welcome the new gadget were the organizers of Harlem's Saturday night rent parties. Meyer Parkoff, who was a juke box dealer at the time, is quoted by John Krivine as follows: 'Rather than hiring a band, they would ask me for a phonograph which I would put in on the Saturday and take out after the weekend. This gave them an additional source of income which helped pay the rent, because they didn't have to pay the band, and they made some money from the juke box. There was a lot of that in those days.'

By the autumn of 1929, Homer Capehart had a range of seven machines, and the following year he announced that he would increase his output to 40,000 machines a year.

In 1933, Farny Wurlitzer, of the celebrated organ family, realized that the repeal of Prohibition would open up a huge market for musical entertainment. He hired Homer Capehart, who had got himself into financial difficulties, and within two years they were selling juke boxes just as fast as they could produce them.

By then, the radio networks, CBS, NBC and, in 1934, a

third one, the Mutual Broadcasting System, had woken up to the fact that they were missing out on a good thing. Dance music, and even out and out jazz, were becoming a staple of their nightly programmes, often in the form of 'remotes' from hotel ballrooms and the larger dance halls. But the appetite of the juke boxes for new material was unassuageable, and record sales began to boom.

Jack Kapp had been able to lure some of the important names away from his old firm, Brunswick, among them Guy Lombardo and Bing Crosby; and one of the first bands he signed was Chick Webb's.

Their first records were released in America late in 1934, and almost simultaneously in Britain. Among them another Edgar Sampson composition, 'Don't Be That Way', with solos for Elmer Williams on tenor, Sampson on alto, Claude Jones on trombone, and Taft Jordan on trumpet. Jordan was an exciting trumpet player, who modelled his style on that of Louis Armstrong, both in his playing and in his singing. He can be heard doing both on another Edgar Sampson arrangement for 'On The Sunny Side Of The Street'.

Kapp's control of the repertoire was absolute. Swing bands like Chick Webb's were permitted to record instrumental numbers such as the Edgar Sampson originals, but outside of that, Decca's hardnosed commercialism demanded that all artists, bands and singers alike, record the popular hits of the day. Jazz musicians suffered miserably from this policy but somehow managed to produce small works of art based on the most commonplace material: witness Louis Armstrong's 'Dear Old Southland', and Fats Waller's 'I'm Gonna Sit Right Down And Write Myself A Letter'.

Ella Fitzgerald made her first record with Chick Webb on June 12th, 1935. The title was 'Love And Kisses', with music by J. C. Johnson and words by George Whiting and Nat Schwartz. It is a song which has since disappeared without trace.

At roughly the same time, at the Brunswick studios,

Teddy Wilson was recording with a pick-up band and 'vocal chorus by Billie Holiday'. He explains how the songs were allocated. 'In those days the publishers made the hits. They had what they called number one, number two and number three plugs – the songs they were pushing. We never got into the plug tunes. We had our choice of the rest. That's why many of the songs we recorded you never heard anybody singing besides Billie.'

Leonard Feather gives us Ella's recollections of her recording of 'Love and Kisses' with the Chick Webb band, in an article he wrote for *Playboy* magazine in 1957. 'I'll never forget it,' said Ella. 'After we made it, the band was in Philadelphia one night when they wouldn't let me in to some beer garden where I wanted to hear it on the piccolo [jukebox]. So I had some fellow who was over twenty-one go in and put a nickel in while I stood outside and listened to my own voice coming out.'

It should be understood that at the time, recordings by Billie Holiday, Ella Fitzgerald, all the other black artists and musicians, were directed at an exclusively black audience. It is true that John Hammond, Leonard Feather and some others, were energetically drawing the attention of white audiences to these 'race records', and that in New York, Chicago, Los Angeles and London, small groups of dedicated jazz fans were beginning to form – nevertheless, the sales of such records were modest when compared to those of such as Bing Crosby, Guy Lombardo and Kate Smith, the real recording stars of their day. But the recording costs were so low that sales of a few thousand were enough to turn a profit for the company responsible for them.

Chick continued to nurse Ella along – slowly, slowly. Choosing her songs, building arrangements around her. There can be no doubt that he was becoming increasingly aware of her rare qualities, but equally at pains not to push her too far, too fast.

Ella proved to be a quick learner. She was still painfully shy, but in the warm and exciting atmosphere of the Savoy, and with a phalanx of friendly musicians behind her, she felt safe and happy; she could lay back on Chick's powerful beat, relax, and sing her heart out.

If Ella became impatient with the pace of her progress, she soon learned to control it. She said: 'I felt I wanted to be a big success in a hurry – and I found that all through the years you never appreciate anything if you get it in a hurry.'

One of the numbers she recorded with the band in 1935 was called 'Rhythm And Romance'. Along with Crosby and the other American Decca stars (Bing had had an enormous hit the year before with 'Love In Bloom'), Edward Lewis was releasing some of the Chick Webb sides in England. *Melody Maker* gave them enthusiastic reviews: '. . . the blend of the sax section on one or two sessions should thrill you to the core – as should Ella's vocals.'

Another of her titles to receive some acclaim was a Sam Coslow song she recorded in October 1936. It was called 'If You Can't Sing It, You'll Have To Swing it', or, as it came to be called, 'Mr Paganini'.

> Mr Paganini,
> Please play my rhapsody,
> And if you cannot play it
> Won't you sing it?
> And if you can't sing it –
> You'll simply have to
> Swing it, I said swing it,
> Oh oh oh, swing it,
> And don't wing it.
>
> Oh, Mr Paganini,
> We breathlessly await,
> Your masterful baton
> Go on and sling it;
> And if you can't sling it,
> You'll simply have to
> Swing it, I said, swing it,
> And scaddy wha, wha,
> And whuddy scat lah.

We've heard your repertoire,
And at the final bar,
We greeted you with wild applause;
But what a great ovation,
Your interpretation,
Bud doodi laddy diddy
Yeh, yeh, yeh.

It may very well have been the first time that Ella had
tried out her talent for scat singing. She had, the boys in the
band had observed, a remarkable ear, and the ability to
imitate almost anything musical that came her way. And
seated as she was, night after night, on the Savoy bandstand
among such musicians as Taft Jordan, Edgar Sampson,
Sandy Williams and Louis Jordan, it was surely inevitable
that she should add scat singing to her array of vocal skills.
Didn't she sing, as Bardu Ali had noted the first time he
heard her, just like a horn?

That year, Chick Webb made his radio debut. He was
awarded a thirty minute weekly broadcast entitled *Gems Of
Colour*, a sort of variety show featuring black acts, all backed
up by Chick and the band, with Ella as the principal vocalist.

Some of Ella's earliest admirers were 3,000 miles away, in
Britain. British fans, an ever-increasing number of them,
were kept informed about jazz happenings on the other side
of the Atlantic by their journals, the weekly *Melody Maker*
and the monthly *Rhythm*. They were told that they could
hear Chick Webb's broadcasts over the General Electric
Company's short wave station at Schenectady, New York.
This they did, enduring the frustration of waves of static
roaring over the ether like the mighty Atlantic itself, sometimes completely obliterating the music. Of one such broadcast, *Melody Maker* wrote: 'In "Frost On The Moon", (Ella)
combines with Charlie Linton, the band's regular male
vocalist, and Louis Jordan in a vocal trio which was almost
inaudible, coming at the worst period of bad reception. By
the time they came to "Honeysuckle Rose" it was possible to
appreciate Ella's grand singing more fully.'

Towards the end of 1936, Ella recorded for the first time under her own name: Ella Fitzgerald and the Savoy Eight. The titles were a venerable jazz standard, 'The Darktown Strutters Ball', and a song made famous by Louis Armstrong some years earlier, 'Shine'. The *Melody Maker* reviewer remarked, 'It is strange that last month, when Chick's name was on the label, Ella Fitzgerald hogged the record, whereas this new one, under her own name, with eight of the Webb band, gives more space to the band. Patchy.' He suggested that the best example of Ella's work to date was 'Mr Pagganinny'. That was the way Ella pronounced the name on the record; clearly she had never heard of the demon fiddler of Genoa.

Whitney Balliet, most respected of jazz commentators, has written: 'The Negro invents, the white man borrows.' Adding (this was 1968): 'Duke Ellington still struggles, while Benny Goodman retires.'

Goodman was one of the white musicians from Chicago and the Middle West who reached New York during the twenties and thirties (Bix Beiderbecke, Eddie Condon, Jimmy McPartland, Gene Krupa and Glenn Miller were others), and found in Harlem the inspiration they were looking for. Jack Teagarden and Tommy Dorsey used to hang around Small's Paradise listening to Jimmy Harrison, a legendary trombone player who died in 1931. Gene Krupa literally sat at the feet of Chick Webb at the Savoy. He considered Chick 'the most luminous of all drum stars, the master'.

There was, of course, no possibility of a white musician playing with a black band; the idea of a black musician in a white band was equally outlandish. Black and white musicians lived and worked in separate worlds, the difference in their status most clearly seen in a comparison of their wages. In 1930, Paul Whiteman, the 'king of jazz', most celebrated of white bandleaders, was paying his key men between $250 and $350 a week; in 1933, Taft Jordan, trumpeter and singer with Chick Webb's band at the Savoy, was earning $35.

Nineteen-year-old Artie Shaw, penniless in New York in 1929, found his way to Harlem and Pod's and Jerry's Catagonia Club. There, Willie 'the Lion' Smith ruled at his piano. 'I soon struck up an acquaintance with him, and after that plucked up enough courage to ask him if I might bring my horn down some night so I could sit in with him. He hesitated, then nodded. That was enough for me. The following night I was back with my horn.' In his autobiography, *The Trouble With Cinderella*, Shaw continued: '. . . my nightly stint at Pod's and Jerry's gave me the one thing I needed to fill in the emptiness of my life at that time, a sense of *belonging* – a feeling of being *accepted*. Within a few nights I could see that the Lion liked the way I played. I continued to come down and sit in every night; and since I had no money at all, he got into the habit of buying me a drink now and then, and some breakfast when we wound up at six, seven, or eight in the morning. Occasionally he might ask me along when he set out after work for some little musicians' hangout that stayed open till noon or even later, where he'd sit down at the piano and tell me to get out my horn in order to show me off to some of his colleagues. Whenever I played something they approved of, he would look arrogantly over at them and announce, "Tha's my boy – you hear that?"'

Benny Goodman was born in Chicago in 1909. A musician of enormous talent, he was already playing the clarinet professionally at the age of twelve. Among his party pieces was his imitation of the then celebrated Ted Lewis. Not the head of English Decca, but the clarinet-playing bandleader, who used to wail in an agonized *sprechgesang*: 'Say, don't you know who I am, with this horn in my hand? Why, I'm that ol' medicine man – for your bloo – ooo – ooze.' By 1929, Goodman was in New York, leading the life of a busy freelance musician, in theatre pits, on radio and on records.

All through those early New York years, with the help of John Hammond, he was organizing bands for recording sessions; bands which included such virtuosi as Jack Teagarden, his brother Charlie, Manny Klein, Joe Sullivan, Dick McDonough, Artie Bernstein and Gene Krupa. By 1934, he was putting together his first big band. The model for it was firmly in his head: it was to sound like the black bands he heard on his nightly prowlings around Broadway and Harlem – Fletcher Henderson, Jimmy Lunceford and Chick Webb.

Charlie Buchanan used to let Benny rehearse his band at the Savoy. 'He wanted to get that rhythm of Chick Webb.' When Chick got to hear of it, he growled, 'You'll never get my rhythm.'

That was the standard reaction of black musicians to white. Even the best of the whites were allowed only grudging and much qualified admiration. Dickie Wells thought that Jack Teagarden could blow: 'He was one of the few really down cats who knew that horn bottom-side up, and he really poured his feelings through it.'

However good a white musician was (he was more highly trained and he played a better instrument), what he didn't do, what he couldn't do – was swing. 'Man, it's a feelin',' Chick Webb is supposed to have said. 'It's like lovin' a special girl, and you don't see her for a year, and then she comes back – it's something inside you. When I'm at the drums, an' I feel the band thick and strong around me, we're swingin'. The crowd feels it, and they're swingin' too.' Which only goes to show how difficult it is to describe. In an odd sort of way the white musicians conceded the point. As Cante Flamenco was to the Andalusian gypsy, so swing was the exclusive territory of urban black Americans.

Benny Goodman asked Charlie Buchanan to hire his band for a night's work at the Savoy. Charlie agreed to do so. 'I'll pay you union scale. Ten dollars a man, and twenty dollars for leaders.'

Benny was appalled. 'You can't do that,' he protested.

'Look, Benny,' said Charlie, 'until you prove to me that you can bring 'em in, that's what I'm going to pay you.' The next time Buchanan hired Goodman for the Savoy, in

1937, he had to pay him three thousand, three hundred dollars for one night.

In December 1934, Benny and his band were booked for a series of network shows, sponsored by the National Biscuit Company, called *Let's Dance*. The shows, which went on the air for five hours every Saturday night, were broadcast all over America, and because of the three-hour time difference from coast to coast, could be heard for the first three hours in New York, while the last three hours could be heard on the West Coast. There were three bands: Xavier Cugat for Latin music, Kel Murray for dance music, and Benny Goodman and his orchestra, the last band on the programme, for jazz.

By the spring of 1935, after six months on the air, the band was playing just the way Goodman had dreamed they might. The arrangements were written (and paid for by the network) by the men he most admired; men like Fletcher Henderson, Jimmy Munday, who wrote for Earl Hines, and Edgar Sampson of Chick Webb's band. Unfortunately, apart from their Saturday night radio stint, the band had no other work. Nobody seemed willing to engage an outfit that played such uncompromising swing music. That might be all right for the noisy dance halls of Harlem, but the polite clientèle of Manhattan's grand hotels and expensive restaurants might find it an intolerable intrusion.

Then Guy Lombardo, who played at the Roosevelt Hotel on Madison Avenue, decided the time had come to take his famous Royal Canadians on a tour of one-night stands. His agents, the Music Corporation of America (MCA), who also represented Benny, thought it might be an idea to try the Goodman band in his place.

John Hammond describes what happened on opening night. 'Customers were sitting at their tables in shock. Waiters were moving through the room with their fingers in their ears, even though Benny's brass section was muted and the band was doing its best to provide the brand of dinner music the Roosevelt clientèle was used to.' Benny lasted just two weeks, after which MCA sent him and the band on tour.

The tour was a disaster. Benny wrote to John Hammond, who was in London. He told him that in Denver the band were made to wear funny hats, and that he himself had been forced to do his Ted Lewis imitation – the same corny routine (battered top hat and clarinet) with which he had entranced his adoring family at the age of twelve!

At last, in August 1935, the band reached the West Coast, where they were booked to appear at the Palomar Ballroom in Los Angeles. In *Hear Me Talking To Ya*, Benny Goodman describes that historic occasion to Nat Shapiro and Nat Hentoff. 'When we opened at the Palomar we had a "what've we got to lose" attitude and decided to let loose and shoot the works with our best things like "Sugar Foot Stomp", "Sometimes I'm Happy", and the others. Actually though, we were almost scared to play. From the moment I kicked them off, the boys dug in with some of the best playing I'd heard since we left New York. I don't know what it was, but the crowd went wild, and then – boom!'

To John Hammond 'what it was' was clear. 'This crowd had heard the late hours of the *Let's Dance* broadcasts, so Benny had fans ready and waiting . . . it was as simple as the three hour difference between New York and Los Angeles.'

Boom! The 'swing era' had begun.

There was another important event that summer. Goodman went into the studio for the first of the Benny Goodman Trio sessions with Gene Krupa and Teddy Wilson. In his *Encyclopedia of Jazz*, Leonard Feather comments: 'By taking Wilson on the road the following spring for personal appearances with the trio as an adjunct to the band, Goodman broke down racial taboos for the first time in jazz history on a large, national scale.' In August 1936, Benny added Lionel Hampton, the great vibraharpist, to the trio, and the grim wall of segregation had been well and truly breached.

At the end of the year, in spite of the fact that Goodman had at last found a girl singer he liked in Helen Ward, he responded to Ella Fitzgerald's growing reputation by engaging her for a recording session. She sang a couple of songs. One of them was by Mack Gordon and Harry Revel:

> Goodnight, my love,
> The tired old moon is descending;
> Goodnight, my love,
> My moment with you dear, is ending.

There was a row over that session. Goodman recorded for RCA Victor, and Ella's contract was with Chick Webb and Decca. 'They had to take my name off the label, because the songs became a hit,' says Ella. 'Because Chick was working with Decca.'

Ella was still not out of her teens, but it is a measure of her new found confidence, notably vis-à-vis her fellow musicians, that she began writing songs. On February 18th 1937, Teddy Wilson's recording session with Billie Holiday included a song composed by Chick Webb, Teddy McRae, tenor player with the band, Benny Green, the trombonist – and with a lyric by Ella Fitzgerald. It was called 'You Showed Me The Way', and it survives along with all the other classic Billie Holiday recordings of that period. The melody is run-of-the-mill popular song writing, but Ella's lyric, while following the Tin Pan Alley love song conventions of the day, does reveal a keen ear for the choice of 'singable' words.

> You showed me the way,
> When I was someone in distress,
> A heart in search of happiness,
> You showed me the way.
>
> My skies were so gray,
> I never knew I'd feel a thrill,
> I couldn't dream a dream until
> You showed me the way.
>
> The moment you found me,
> The shadows around me

Just disappeared from view;
The world became rosy,
Each corner so cosy,
Darling, all because of you.

You showed me the way,
And I've learned that love can be
A paradise for you and me,
Here's all I can say –
You showed me the way.

Ella continued to write songs, picking out the tunes with one finger on the piano. In 1940, she wrote words to Duke Ellington's melody, 'In A Mellotone', and in 1945, Nat 'King' Cole recorded another of her efforts, 'Oh, But I Do'. In 1943, she had done enough to gain membership of ASCAP, the American Society of Composers, Authors and Publishers. She was the youngest person ever to do so.

The following month, because Billie was out of town with Jimmy Lunceford, Ella stepped in as her deputy. To have agreed to do that must surely represent yet another giant step in professional aplomb. 'Well, I got a little rise in salary,' says Ella. 'I got a chance to get a little more money than I was getting, which was nothing at the time.'

And she was getting lots of offers. In April she recorded with the Mills Brothers. This vocal act: father John, and his three sons, Herbert, Harry and Donald had been national favourites since 1931, and their visit to England in 1934 had turned them into international stars with numerous imitators. John had joined the act when his eldest son, John Junior, had died in 1936. The only musical accompaniment was John's four-stringed guitar – with Herbert, Donald and Harry singing three part harmony, and John supplying a vocal bass line. This was a period of increasingly sophisticated amplification systems, and the four Mills Brothers, grouped around a non-directional microphone, could really make themselves sound as crisp and swingy as a full-sized band.

The *Melody Maker* reviewer greeted the records warmly: 'The Fitzgerald-Mills combination of talent was a brilliant notion in one respect: it brings out the very best in Ella. With this quiet background and a fairly good tune in "Big Boy Blue", she turns in a really grand performance.'

'Big Boy Blue' may have been 'a fairly good tune', but it still wasn't a 'number one plug' in Teddy Wilson's definition. Of all the songs recorded by Ella in 1937, not one is remembered. Here are some of the titles: 'Love, You're Just A Laugh', 'Gee, But You're Swell', 'All Over Nothing At All', 'Somewhere Deep In the Heart Of The South', and 'When I Get High I Get Low'.

In June, Chick Webb and his band, with Ella Fitzgerald, left the Savoy Ballroom for a five week tour of one-night stands.

Maxine Sullivan, who became a star in 1937 when she sang a cute and swingy version of 'Loch Lomond', had this to say on the subject of touring: 'I often wondered how Ella and Helen Humes [with Count Basie] and the other singers could *do* the one-night stand thing, year after year. I did it once with Benny Carter and when I got back to New York, I kissed the *ground*.'

It was no better for the musicians. And for the big bands, touring was an absolute necessity. Whether your home base was New York, Chicago or Los Angeles, as soon as an engagement in hotel or ballroom ended, there was nothing for it but to hit the road. In no other way could so expensive an outfit as a big swing band be held together. Sometimes a band would land a job – a week, two weeks, a month – at some Mid western or West Coast ballroom, but more often than not, touring meant a gruelling succession of one-nighters.

Fletcher Henderson, who adored big, fast cars, encouraged his musicians to travel in this way, but most bands had a bus, usually bearing the band's name along its side, and the legend 'On Tour'. After several thousand miles of bad roads, such vehicles had often reduced themselves to piles of exhausted malodorous junk.

Ironically, the dates most available to the black bands were on the campuses of Southern Universities, where the white collegiates were demanding to dance to the bands they'd been hearing on the radio and on records. It was a jolting experience for musicians accustomed to the easy come, easy go atmosphere of Harlem.

Dickie Wells, who toured with Fletcher Henderson,

wrote: 'In those days, when we were travelling in the South, most cats had firearms somewhere, somehow. Because you used to run up against a lot of frightful people, drunken people, and what not. The ofays would try to frighten you if somebody got out of line, and want to beat up the band or shoot somebody. If you pull a gun, there's two chances to one the cat is going to cool down. It's a fool who's going to keep messing with you after he sees this gun. . . . Somebody always seems to think a musician on a bandstand is a woman's man, and he just hates you for that, so the best you can do is rub him down or fan him. You don't have time to make love to everybody! Or maybe you're a friendly guy, just going around shaking hands, trying to look neat and your best, as the public wants you to. You'd be surprised how a lot of guys figure you're acting cute and trying to be something else.'

'Ofay' was the Harlem word for white man. It is probably pig-Latin or back-slang for 'foe'. Black musicians had no illusions about what faced them when they crossed the Mason-Dixon line; they were entering enemy territory. 'To show you how things were,' says Taft Jordan. 'You'd play towns where you'd have four or five thousand people there, and you couldn't find a place to eat. One time in Columbia, Tennessee, you had to go to the back of the place, they'd serve you out of a window at the back. And the police came along and made 'em stop serving out of the window. Tough.'

In many ways, the Northern States and the Midwest were no better, and in some ways, worse. James Haskins, writing about Lena Horne touring with Noble Sissle and his band in 1935, noted: 'In the Midwestern towns where they played, there were no sizable black communities, and thus few friendly boarding-houses or restaurants. Their tour bus became their hotel ... In Terre Haute, Indiana, they were forced to spend the night in the grounds of the Clyde Beatty Circus.'

As Taft Jordan said, 'Tough.' The musicians kept themselves going the best way they could. Dickie Wells again: 'You may play a beautiful ballroom in Alabama or Mississippi, and maybe you've travelled four or five hundred miles getting there, and people are crazy about you while you are on the bandstand. There's a big restaurant next door, but when you've finished playing they won't serve you. But they'll give you whisky, all the whisky you want.... That had a lot to do with musicians drinking. I know it had.'

Louis Armstrong complained: 'When I was coming along, a black man had hell. On the road he couldn't find no decent place to eat, sleep, or use the toilet – service station cats see a bus of coloured bandsmen drive up and they would sprint to lock their rest-room doors.'

Ella Fitzgerald seems to have had no such problems. She loved being with the band, and they in their turn protected her, fussed over her and shielded her from the humiliations which were their daily experience on the road. She was young, she was full of life and she enjoyed every minute of it. She remembers: 'When we'd get to a town, instead of going to sleep, or resting like a young lady, I'd be out playing baseball, or something – throwing ball. And they'd say, you gotta stop that – you've got to act like a young lady.' In order to play a more active role in the life of the band, she decided to learn to play the piano accordion. Sadly, she soon had to abandon the effort: 'I couldn't carry [the accordion] and the fellers in the band got tired of lugging it around, so that was the end of that.'

The magazine *Down Beat* had begun to publish in 1935, partly as a trade paper for musicians and others engaged in the business of making music, but also in response to a new audience who were simply fascinated by bands, their leaders and their side-men. These readers wanted to know everything: who was playing where, who had left what band to join what other band. For the first time, the side-men, the rank and file instrumentalists, and this was especially true of the black musicians, became real people, with names, nicknames, families and birthdays. The manufacturers of musical instruments suddenly assumed magical identities: Selmer saxophones, Conn trumpets, Ludwig drums, Epiphone and Gibson guitars, all became names to conjure with. It was readers of *Down Beat* who, in the next five years,

48

would help create fortunes for bandleaders like Benny Goodman, the Dorsey Brothers, Artie Shaw and Glenn Miller.

One of the first things *Down Beat* did was to institute popularity polls to determine who was the best player on every instrument in the band. The results were published in the first issue of every year, and in 1937, Ella Fitzgerald was voted the best girl vocalist. At the end of that year, *Melody Maker* in London echoed the compliment. Ella was voted top with 518 votes; Mildred Bailey second with 417 votes, and third, with 391 votes, was Billie Holiday.

Ella would undoubtedly not have endorsed this judgement; more probably she would have been acutely embarrassed by it. For among the 'fem chirpers', or 'gal yippers', as *Down Beat* dismissively dubbed them, Billie Holiday was the queen. In fact, during another tour with Chick in 1938, Ella would spend a great deal of time at the Roseland State Ballroom in Boston, listening to Billie sing with Artie Shaw.

According to John Chilton, 'Billie did not feel jealous of Ella's success and her subsequent popular adulation; she learned to shrug off any comparisons and poll-placings. However, she felt keen disappointment in 1939 when the leading journalists of the Associated Negro Press voted Ella their favourite female vocalist and chose Maxine Sullivan in second place.'

Something else happened during that visit to Boston. One day, Ella was seated at the piano, playing a one-finger melody, and singing. It was a nursery song that she had known all her life – 'We used to use it as a game at school.'

> A-Tisket, A-Tasket,
> A brown and yellow basket,
> I sent a letter to my mummy,
> On the way I dropped it.
> I dropped it, I dropped it,
> Yes, on the way I dropped it,
> A little girlie picked it up
> And put it in her pocket.

Al Feldman was a young pianist who had been arranging for Chick Webb for a couple of years. (He would later change his name to Van Alexander and have a good career as a band-leader.) He listened to Ella singing to her own one-finger accompaniment, and remarked that what she was doing would make a cute little novelty number. Well, novelty numbers were all the rage that year. Hadn't Claude Thorn-hill done wonders for Maxine Sullivan with his arrangement of 'Loch Lomond'? And there was Larry Clinton's 'The Dipsy Doodle', there was 'Knock, Knock, Who's There?', and the hallucinatory nonsense of Slim Gaillard and Slam Stewart's 'The Flat Foot Floogie With the Floy Floy'.

Basing songs on familiar folk material was also a popular thing to do. Rudy Vallee had just had a substantial hit with his version of a Yale University drinking song, with echoes of Rudyard Kipling's poem 'Gentlemen Rankers', called 'The Whiffenpoof Song'. Ella herself had only recently recorded a cover version of the Andrews Sisters' Yiddish flavoured hit, 'Bei Mir Bist Du Schoen'.

Ella and Al Feldman fooled around with 'A-Tisket' some more, and together they came up with a song. 'We tried it out in Boston,' says Ella, 'and everybody liked it. I guess because of the game they played, you know?' Chick Webb liked it too, and when the band got back to New York, he decided to record it.

At Decca, Jack Kapp was unimpressed. 'What is it?' he complained. 'It's just a children's song. Kids' stuff. Who's gonna buy that?' Chick argued, and the band backed him up. For one thing, on recording sessions, the musicians got paid five dollars a side. Four sides, twenty dollars. If they didn't record they didn't get paid. And there was time for one more side.

Chick Webb made the decision: 'We're gonna record this tune.' And they did.

Was it green?
No, no, no, no!
Was it red?

50

No, no, no, no!
Was it blue?
No, no, no, no!
Just a little yellow basket.

That summer, 'A-Tisket, A-Tasket' became a smash hit. By September, the record had sold a million copies and was number one on the U.S. Hit Parade. Later, Ella would wistfully remark that had they been awarding gold discs in those days she'd have got one. Fats Waller recorded a cover version of the song, and that too was a hit. Both as a singer and as a song writer, Ella Fitzgerald was famous.

Chick Webb reacted to his singer's new status by featuring her more and more. 'He never felt he was the only star,' says Ella. 'Anyone who could do something, he gave them the chance to do it.' He had arrangements made to show her off at her very best. 'Which was funny in a way,' said Taft Jordan. 'Because she would have made anybody's arrangements sound good.'

Ella had started work at the Savoy at a salary of $25 a week, which Chick had since raised to $50. But her new celebrity was causing problems. Benny Goodman was interested in her, and so was Jimmy Lunceford, who offered her $75. Chick Webb countered that bid by upping the ante to $125. At a time when the average weekly wage was around $35, that was a fortune.

Ella's newly won fame and unaccustomed affluence may have been the cause of one of her few major indiscretions: she got married. Talking to Leonard Feather many years later, she confessed. 'I went out and got married on a bet, I was that stupid. The guy bet me I wouldn't marry him.' (When Feather asked her to name the man she had married, she had some difficulty recalling it.) When she came back and told the boys in the band what she had done, they were appalled. As her legal guardian, Chick Webb insisted that the damage be undone. Within days Ella was in court, having the marriage annulled. She recalls: 'And the judge told me, "You just keep singing 'A-Tisket A-Tasket' and leave those men alone." '

The band began to change. It was Chick Webb and his band with Ella Fitzgerald; and sometimes it was even billed as Ella Fitzgerald with the Chick Webb band. This new emphasis may have pleased the general public, but it saddened the true blue Chick Webb fans. Reviewing a new record in March 1939, a *Melody Maker* critic, in elegiac mood, wrote: 'Presenting the decline and fall of William Webb Esquire. This band has now reached a stage where one feels that everything it plays has the express object of pleasing those audiences that have been roped in by the attraction of Ella's personality and are not otherwise interested in jazz.

'The arrangements and the performances have lost that looseness, i.e. that swing of the best Webb days. They are packed with clichés and self-conscious effects. The rhythm section has declined, the sax section has what the divorce courts call incompatibility of temperament. If you don't believe me, play this after one of Webb's old ones – or, even better, the early Fitzgerald period, "I'll Chase The Blues Away", and "A Little Bit Later On".

'All you get on the new disc is a good trumpet solo on both sides plus a lot of arranging that means nothing. "Got A Pebble In My Shoe" is such an irritatingly childish piece of affectation that it embarrasses me to play it.... Though still clinging to my affection for Ella's original "Tisket", I have realized now what the result of all this commercial success has been. It's the old and regrettable story. After hearing this record, I said, "Thank heavens for Basie." '

The pressure to become more commercial came expressly from the Decca Record Company, in the person of a new Artists and Repertoire man named Milt Gabler. Gabler recorded Louis Armstrong for years, and was a jazz buff of impeccable credentials – he ran Sunday afternoon jam sessions at Jimmy Ryan's on 52nd Street, and owned the Commodore Music Shop. But at Decca he was all A and R man, and as such, was determined to exploit Ella's new

52

celebrity. His main preoccupation with his black artists was to ensure that they recorded what was called 'cross-over music', music which would lift them from their purely 'race' orientation, and heighten their appeal for white audiences. In a radio interview, Milt Gabler explained how it worked: 'Back in those days the A and R man was the boss, and the artist knew that we were right on the scene with all the new songs. In those days, don't forget, the artists didn't write their own material. The publishers would have songs that they were working on and plugging, that you hear on radio broadcasts for the next ninety days period, and we knew that certain publishers were investing a lot of money in plugging songs on programmes and clubs and radio stations. We analysed the song, and it had a very good chance of becoming a hit, so we would have everything waiting for them – and they didn't see the song until they came into the studio – from Bing Crosby all the way to Ella Fitzgerald, and everyone else.'

In January 1939, Ella won the *Down Beat* poll for the third year in succession. She also won a similar poll in *Metronome*, a magazine which hitherto had concerned itself only with more 'serious' music, but now began devoting its pages more and more to the swing bands that had begun to proliferate since Benny Goodman's spectacular debut only four years earlier.

Most successful of the post-Goodman bands was Glenn Miller's. Miller, a thirty-five-year-old trombonist and arranger, had hit upon a unique way of voicing his saxophone section (clarinet lead over two altos and two tenors), and with recordings like 'Moonlight Serenade', 'In The Mood', and 'Little Brown Jug', his band was enormously popular. In fact, in 1939, all the white swing bands – Artie Shaw, Tommy Dorsey, Jimmy Dorsey, Charlie Barnet, and Woody Herman – were firmly in command. Their records were selling by the million, their leaders were rich and famous.

And Chick Webb and his band were on the road again.

It was early summer when Chick's frail body at last succumbed to the rigours of the life he had chosen to lead. The band was playing a hotel date in some Southern town. One of the musicians went to the manager and asked if there was a place where Chick could lie down. 'Sure,' said the manager. 'He can lie down in the closet where we keep the brooms.'

The band was playing on a riverboat outside Washington when Chick collapsed again. He was rushed to Johns Hopkins hospital for an operation. And when the tuberculosis of the spine which had bedevilled his short life proved to be inoperable, they got him to the home of his parents in Baltimore. For a whole week he fought for his life, his bed surrounded by friends and relatives. On Friday, June 16th 1939, he asked his mother to lift him up. 'I'm sorry,' he said. 'I gotta go.' And then he died.

The band, who had continued the tour ('no play, no pay, guys'), were in Montgomery, Alabama when they got the news. They went to Baltimore for the funeral. Chick's body was laid out for inspection, a somewhat macabre custom in those parts, that some of the band found 'sort of primitive'. Many musicians came, both black and white. Taft Jordan remembers, 'Gene Krupa was there, breaking down. He came to view Chick's remains. He idolized Chick.'

The funeral itself was, by all accounts, a highly emotional occasion. According to the *Daily Mirror*, which had picked up an agency report: 'Thousands of hysterical mourners sobbingly intoned the blues tunes most associated with Chick's band. His boys played a jazz requiem, and during the burial service, the coffin was submerged in flowers.'

Ella stood beside the coffin and sang a song written by Gus Kahn and Walter Donaldson in 1922. Corny though it was, it expressed to perfection her sense of irretrievable loss.

> Nights are long since you went away,
> I think about you all through the day,
> My buddy,
> My buddy,
> No buddy quite so true.

Miss your voice, the touch of your hand,
Just long to know that you understand,
My buddy,
My buddy,
Your buddy misses you.

Frank Schiffman, the owner of the Apollo Theatre, said, 'The most moving thing I ever heard was Ella singing "My Buddy" over Webb's casket. Even those who barely knew the man wept.' And Moe Gale said, 'There were thousands of people. It was the biggest funeral I had ever seen – and I know there wasn't a dry eye when Ella sang.'

'He was always in pain, but no one ever knew it,' said Ella, of the little drummer who had done so much for her. 'If he'd have taken the same time that he applied to helping people, and rested, he'd have lived longer than his twenty-nine years. And there was so much music in that man.'

Like many another black musician, Chick Webb was never certain of his own age. Ella has him twenty-nine when he died; others have him born in 1902, and thus thirty-seven. And the *Melody Maker* obituary, an exercise in the purest bathos, had yet another opinion: 'Thirty-two years ago, in a humble Baltimore shack, a small, insignificant hunchbacked ball of brown skinned flesh was born.(!) As the ball grew into childhood, he looked so tiny and frail, his mother called him Chick. For many years he was her chick, rushing under her protective wings whenever danger threatened. For Mrs Webb's son never could take care of himself as a youngster. Even his father shook his head and murmured, "He'll never do any good, he ain't got no muscle."'

After the funeral, the band sat around feeling lost. They were like a bereaved family. Where did they go from here? Moe Gale came and talked to them. 'Look,' he said. 'Chick, who we all loved, has gone. But Chick Webb's band is still a going concern. Charlie Buchanan still wants you at the Savoy. Milt Gabler wants to go on recording you at Decca. Big bands are in demand. So why don't you stay together?

The Gale Agency will look after you. We'll see you get lots of work.'

That sounded okay. But the big question remained – if the band was to stay together, who was going to be the leader? Who was going to be the boss? Well now, the answer to that was obvious, wasn't it? Who, for the past year, had Chick been so carefully grooming, featuring more and more, to the point where a lot of their old true blue jazz fans had started to complain? Ella Fitzgerald. Who else?

It was true. It was almost as if little Chick had planned it so; had foreseen his own departure and elected his successor. As if to confirm this sombre notion, Decca at once put out a Chick Webb Memorial Album: ten sides. *Melody Maker* reviewed it thus: 'If any ratification is required for my theory of the decline of Chick's band, here it is. Several tracks are leftovers from the sessions which would never have been released but for his death. Eight out of the ten sides are commercial tunes; eight of the ten are sung by Ella.'

And so, Ella Fitzgerald and her orchestra went back to their cosy bandstand at the Savoy. 'She was,' said *Down Beat*, 'one of the youngest big name bandleaders in the world.' 'I really didn't direct the band that much,' said Ella. 'I wasn't of age to be a leader. They had Bardu direct.' And added with characteristic modesty: 'They let me feature one or two numbers.' She had just turned twenty-one.

When Chick Webb died in June 1939, an English reporter had added a footnote to his obituary: 'Incidentally, now that Ella is without a band, how about a visit to this country?' The thought perished on the page; on September 1st, the German army marched into Poland, and two days later England was at war. It would be a long time before the Atlantic would be crossed at the behest of jazz-hungry British fans.

The New York scene was changing too. The big band bonanza, inaugurated in 1935 by Benny Goodman, was beginning to falter. Leonard Feather, in his *Encyclopedia of*

Greatest SHOW VALUE in Harlem

HARLEM
OPERA HOUSE

125th St. west of 7th Ave. Phone UN-4-8519

ONE WEEK — BEGINNING FRIDAY, FEBRUARY 15TH

Tiny
Bradshaw
And His Sensational BAND

MAE ALIX—EDDIE HUNTER—BILLY HIGGINS
3 SAMS—GEORGE BOOKER—ELLA FITZGERALD

Special Added Attraction
MAE WHITMAN Presents
POPS AND LOUIE
WITH ALICE WHITMAN
in a wonderful new act

On the Screen **"MENACE"** Mystery Melodrama | First Chapter **"Rustlers of Red Dog"**

ONE WEEK ONLY — BEGINNING FRIDAY, FEB. 22ND
GREATEST EVENT IN THEATRICAL HISTORY!

CAB CALLOWAY
AND HIS COTTON CLUB ORCHESTRA

AND THE ENTIRE
COTTON CLUB
REVUE

with the great COTTON CLUB Cast:

Nicholas Bros.
Meers & Meers
Lethia Hill
Swann & Lee
Dynamite Hooker
Bill Bailey
Lena Horne
Cora La Redd
Cotton Club
Chorus

Ella's first professional engagement, a week at the Harlem Opera
House in 1935. Note Lena Horne's billing the following week

Ella in 1937: 'I was a real skinny kid'

Hollywood 1942. Ella's first film, *Ride 'Em Cowboy*, with Abbott and Costello. The quartet are the Merry Macs

The Chick Webb Band at the Apollo Theatre in 1937. At the microphone with Ella is Charlie Linton, Chick's male vocalist

Ella's first visit to England in 1948. Extreme left, her brand new husband, Ray Brown. Far right, pianist Hank Jones. On his left, Charlie Short, the English welcoming committee

On the road again: Ella in a Paris dressing room

1954. Ella celebrates her nineteenth anniversary in the music business. Among the celebrants, Eartha Kitt, Dizzy Gillespie (hidden), Charlie Shavers, Louis Bellson, D. L. Hibbler and Pearl Bailey

The late forties. Mr and Mrs Ray Brown

Ella at the microphone: an appreciative Dizzy Gillespie, a watchful Ray Brown

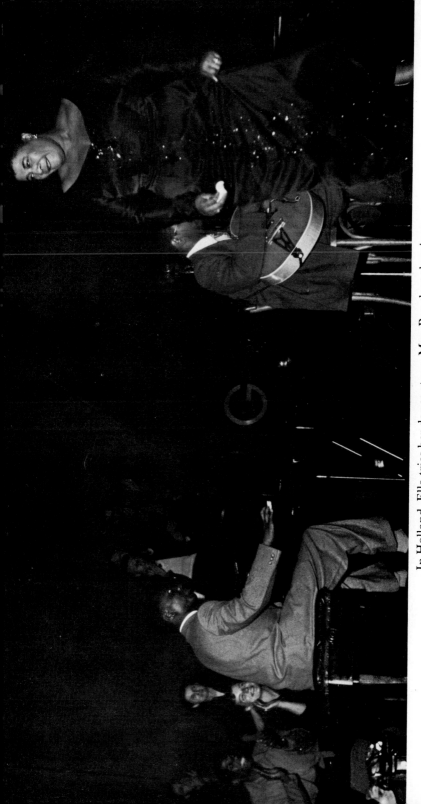

In Holland. Ella tries her dance steps. Max Roach at the piano

'The Cole Porter Songbook', 1956

Jazz, has written: 'By 1939 the market was flooded with swing bands. Many of them, like Harry James', came to rely more on insipid commercial performances than on real swinging jazz for their success. Even a second-rate band could by now give a passable imitation of the Goodman or Lunceford ensembles. The only unique sounds and the only completely inimitable orchestral units in jazz seemed to be those of Duke Ellington and Count Basie. Jazz, to some extent, had reached a stalemate as the 1930s drew to a close.'

In *Down Beat*, in April 1940, Paul Eduard Miller wrote: 'The public is now saturated; most swing bands prior to '39 have made good financially ... as for the rest, even those organized years ago, their financial success, to put it optimistically, is only mediocre.' He stressed the particular predicament of the black swing bands: 'The truth is that the public will only absorb a very limited number of negro bands.' And added: 'Ella Fitzgerald, et cetera, are practically out of the picture as far as the public is concerned.'

However, small-band jazz was enjoying something of a renaissance in the basement clubs which had opened up, usually in premises that had once housed speakeasies, all along 52nd Street. Stuff Smith, a frenetic violinist who played an amplified instrument, took a sextette into the Onyx Club, and became famous with a nonsense song called 'I'se A Muggin''; Wingy Manone, a one-armed trumpet player, was a hit close by at the Famous Door, and it was there that Ella took her band in February 1940 for a short engagement.

There followed a few weeks at the Roseland Ballroom, but before that, there was a trip up north once more to Baltimore, which city was about to honour its native son with a memorial show in aid of the Chick Webb Memorial Recreation Centre Fund. The Governor of Maryland, the State Senator, and nine thousand other Baltimoreans were there, and *Down Beat* reported that the show had been a huge success. 'Joe Louis sat next to the Governor. Ella Fitzgerald, seated beside Chick Webb's widow said, "What Chick did for me and the boys, can never be repaid. The fellows in the band and I can only hope our small contribution will help make Chick Webb's dream come true." Ella and the band's version of "Oh, Johnny" brought Chick's grandad up on stage. He is a boot-black in a Baltimore shoe store, and swings a solid soft shoe of his own. The Ink Spots brought the house down with their recorded favourites; Peg Leg Bates did his dance; the Nicholas Brothers added their contribution, as did Teddy Hill. At 1 a.m., "Auld Lang Syne" reminded us that the New York train wouldn't wait, and thus ended one of the greatest tributes ever paid to a musician. 8000 persons paid $1.15 each, making a fat $9,200 gross.'

But for Ella Fitzgerald and her orchestra, work was becoming harder and harder to find. Even the Lindy-hoppers at the Savoy had found another hero, and Erskine Hawkins, a florid trumpet player from Birmingham, Alabama, who had made a thunderous hit of his version of 'Tuxedo Junction', was the new favourite.

Several attempts were made to reorganize the band. Teddy McRae, the tenor player, who had been appointed the band's musical director, persuaded Edgar Sampson to come back, and Edgar immediately produced a hit for Ella with a song by two Paul Whiteman alumni, Frank Signorelli and Matt Malneck, and words by the 'Stardust' lyricist, Mitchell Parish. The song was 'Stairway To The Stars', and the recording, in which Ella sings two complete choruses, is evidence of the way the singer had come to dominate the band's performances.

Then Teddy McRae left and was replaced as M.D. by another saxophonist/arranger named Eddie Barefield. Sy Oliver, Jimmy Lunceford's brilliant arranger, then busily employed giving Tommy Dorsey's new band its distinctive sound, was asked to join but turned down the offer. Moe Gale tried to persuade Ella to disband the ex-Chick Webbers and join Benny Carter's band, but Ella regarded this as an act of betrayal, and refused. The Gale Agency announced that the Ella Fitzgerald and the Benny Carter bands would continue as separate organizations 'for the time being'.

Well, things were bad all over. In July, the Cotton Club, which had moved uptown in 1936 to Broadway and 48th Street, closed its doors, and so did the Famous Door on 52nd Street. Both clubs owed their musicians money, and James Petrillo of the Musicians' Union stepped in to demand payment. Both Ella and Teddy Powell, bandleader at the Cotton Club, were out of pocket.

All of which left Ella with no alternative but to hit the road again.

There can be little doubt about Ella Fitzgerald's popularity in 1940. In January, *Down Beat* announced its poll winners, and once again Ella came out top canary. Mildred Bailey, first of the white girls fully to be accepted as a jazz singer, came second, and Billie Holiday, whom many, not least Ella herself, considered nonpareil among their kind, came third. Publicists had begun to call Ella 'the first lady of song', and the appellation stuck.

Touring the South that summer, she was granted ample evidence of her celebrity. Leaving the stage of the New Rhythm Club in New Orleans, she was mobbed by four thousand excited black fans, who practically tore off her clothes in their eagerness to move close enough to get an autograph. It was reported: 'Many were knocked down, several others were trampled, and wild confusion reigned. Police were called in an attempt to maintain order.'

The band was now billed as Ella Fitzgerald and her Famous Orchestra, but although Bobby Stark, the trumpet player, and Hilton Jefferson and Wayman Carver on saxophones, three of the star players, had all left, it was still the old Chick Webb band in all but name. The line-up for the 1940 tour was as follows: Taft Jordan, Dick Vance and Irving Randolph, trumpets; George Matthews, John Haughton and Sandy Williams, trombones. Chauncey Haughton and Eddie Barefield, alto saxophones; Lonnie Simmons and Teddy McRae (he'd come back), tenors.

Roger Ramirez, piano, John Trueheart, guitar, Beverly Peers, bass, and Bill Beason, drums.

By the time the band reached Detroit in September, Ella and her band had travelled 18,000 miles and visited thirty-six states. Then it was back to New York to record twenty-six sides for Decca in a single week. The titles included Ella's own compositions 'Just One Of Those Nights', and 'Serenade To A Sleeping Beauty'.

Another short spell at the Savoy was followed in November by an engagement at the Tropicana Club. As the name suggests, the Tropicana was heavily into Latin-American music, and although the rhumbas and tangos were the province of the other band, led by Alberto Socarros, it is a measure of the shortage of suitable dates which must have led the Gale Agency to book Ella and her band there.

The year ended with the Chicago-published *Esquire* magazine announcing 'Carlton Smith's Ten Outstanding Platters For 1940' – number one on his list was 'Gulf Coast Blues' recorded by Ella Fitzgerald and her Famous Orchestra. The song had a distinguished jazz pedigree; it was written by Clarence Williams, the New Orleans pianist and composer of such classics as 'Royal Garden Blues' and 'I Ain't Gonna Give You None Of My Jelly Roll', and it was one of the first songs recorded by Bessie Smith, in February 1923. The record, one of Columbia's 'race series', was released in June of that year and was a huge success, selling, it is said, three quarters of a million copies, a phenomenal hit for those days.

> The mail man passed but he didn't leave no news.
> The mail man passed but he didn't leave no news.
> I'll tell the world,
> He left me with those Gulf Coast blues.

Referring to Ella's version, Carlton Smith called her 'an under-rated blues singer', and suggested that she 'should be heard more often'. Edgar Jackson, in *Melody Maker*, welcomed the record warmly: 'Those who remember Clarence Williams' tuneful "Gulf Coast Blues" will not be the only ones who will enjoy this latest record of it by Ella Fitzgerald. The version may not have the primitive guts (forgive the word but it's so right for the occasion) of the old Bessie Smith waxing, but Ella sings better than she has for a couple of years or more, and the improved musicianship of her band makes the accompaniment worthy of her work.'

But the band's popularity continued to decline. *Down Beat*'s January 1941 poll listed twenty-three bands and Ella's was not among them. And because she was now a bandleader, she was deemed ineligible to compete as best girl singer. That distinction went to twenty-one-year-old Helen O'Connell, the singer with Jimmy Dorsey's band and responsible for such hits as 'Amapola', 'Green Eyes' and 'Tangerine'.

The white swing bands were setting the pace, and curiously, the black bands, under constant pressure from their white managements, were being made to follow. One record reviewer observed: 'Note how the Fitzgerald outfit sounds more white with every new release. The Webb touch is gradually, but surely, slipping away into memory.'

In June, Ella and the band headed for the West Coast. They were to appear at the Orpheum Theatre in Hollywood, and Ella had landed what was described as a featured part in a film starring Abbott and Costello, called *Ride 'Em Cowboy*. She was to play the part a maid, sing her famous hit, 'A-Tisket, A-Tasket', and a song called 'Rockin' And Reelin'', with a popular close harmony act called The Merry Macs.

As the shooting progressed at the Universal Studios, *Down Beat* reported that Ella was getting a great kick out of her first experience as a screen actress, and that she was displaying 'a surprising flair for comedy'. According to that journal, whose expertise, one must remember, was in music rather than movie making – 'Ella turned out to have so much talent in front of the cameras that the bigwigs at Universal have fattened her role with plenty of good lines and footage.'

The role of the coloured maid to which Ella had been assigned was more or less typical of the characterization of Negroes as menials which was the norm for Hollywood in those days. Bill 'Bojangles' Robinson was a shoe-shine boy, the Nicholas Brothers were Pullman porters, and even Eddie Anderson, in his famous portrayal of Rochester, was allowed certain liberties as manservant to Jack Benny, only because of his enormous popularity on the radio.

It is interesting that, a few months later, the climate suddenly and dramatically changed. Both MGM and Twentieth Century Fox produced lavish musicals with all-Negro casts; the one, *Cabin In The Sky*, the other, *Stormy Weather*. An article appeared in the *New York Times* which suggested that these films had been made at the behest of Washington, who were anxious to recruit blacks into the rapidly expanding war industries. The article went on to state that 'the Administration felt that its program for increased employment of Negro citizens in certain heretofore restricted fields of industry would be helped by a general distribution of important pictures in which Negroes played a major part.'

It is just conceivable that *Ride 'Em Cowboy* may have been modified to respond to the governmental edict, and that the fattening of Ella's role was Universal's way of responding to it.

By 1946, with the exigencies of the war years behind them, the Hollywood Studios resumed their bad habits. They once again bowed to the requirements of the Southern exhibitors that Negroes be portrayed in the old degrading ways. James Haskins, in his book about Lena Horne (she had appeared successfully in both *Cabin In The Sky* and *Stormy Weather*), writes: 'The best example of Southern censorship was the reception in Tennessee of *Ziegfeld Follies*, which reached that state in the summer of 1946. The stars were, in order of listing: Fred Astaire, William Powell, Lucille Ball, Lucille Bremer, Fanny Brice, Judy Garland, Kathryn Grayson, Lena Horne, Gene Kelly, James Melton, Victor Moore, Red Skelton and Esther Williams. It featured another nine performers. But when the film reached Knoxville, Tennessee, Emil Bernstecker, the city's reigning theatre magnate, cut all the scenes in which Lena appeared, since they "might prove objectionable to some people in Knoxville." Since Lena's name had been used in most advertisements of the picture, someone in Knoxville had to black out her name on all the posters. In Memphis, no formal announcement was made, but Lena's sequence was deleted from the film for all showings in the city.'

It would be the sixties, and films like Sidney Poitier in Norman Jewison's *In the Heat of the Night*, before black actors and actresses would have achieved full status as mature and responsible human beings.

That summer of '43, Los Angeles enjoyed its greatest musical boom. The bands of Duke Ellington, Jimmy Lunceford, Woody Herman, Bob Crosby and Charlie Barnet all visited the city, and although Ella's band did not appear in *Ride 'Em Cowboy*, Moe Gale had booked them into some of Hollywood's nightspots, so that they all might work together after each day's shooting. When the film was completed, they headed back east.

Ella's recordings that year continued to be uninspired, run-of-the-mill sort of stuff. She had one near hit with a comedy number called 'The Five O'Clock Whistle'.

The five o'clock whistle's on the blink,
The whistle won't blow and what do you think?
My pappy's still in the factory,
Cos he don't know what time it happens to be.

And another with 'Muffin Man'. The Gale Agency issued a press hand-out announcing that Ella had 'responded to requests for phonograph records to be used in London bomb shelters, sending the first hundred recordings of her newest hit "Muffin Man" to the Drury Lane section of the wartorn city.'

The band continued to change. Apart from the normal

63

restlessness of musicians, the Selective Training and Service Act of 1940, the draft, had already begun to pick off the odd side-man here and there, and nobody in their twenties knew where the next blow might fall. Towards the end of 1943, Ella's band acquired a new trumpet player. He was a young man from South Carolina named Dizzy Gillespie.

Dizzy had just left Cab Calloway's band after a fight with his boss which has entered jazz folklore. After a performance in Hartford, Connecticut, Cab accused Dizzy of throwing spitballs on the stage. Dizzy hotly denied it, and there was a scuffle during which Dizzy pulled a knife. Legend has it that he nicked Cab in the backside, but Milton Hinton, the bass player, who was there, has it otherwise. 'The knife had gone into his thigh. And then he looked, and where he had been scuffling, Dizzy had kinda scratched his waist a little with the blade. Not too much, but just a little bit. But the blade had done in his thigh, and that pretty white suit [Cab Calloway's habitual stage costume] was ruined, you know.'

Dizzy was fired on the spot, and right after that he joined Ella. In his autobiography, *To Be Or Not To Bop*, Dizzy writes: 'I played a couple of weeks with them in a place called Lavarge's in Boston, and then came back to New York. That stint with Ella Fitzgerald was pretty funny too, because at first Teddy McRae was the leader who took charge of everything. Ella just sang. It was Ella's band, and the money went to the Gale Agency, which paid Ella, but the musical directorship of the band was in the hands of Teddy McRae and he hired me for those two weeks. After that, they fired him, and Taft Jordan, a trumpet player, took over the band. And so I was no longer with Ella's band after that.'

In any event, Dizzy Gillespie had other things on his mind. Soon, he and a few other young musicians would have invented a new tonal and harmonic language which would sweep the swing bands from the musical map. And profoundly influence the course of Ella Fitzgerald's career.

On December 7th, the Japanese air force bombed Pearl Harbour.

Now the demands of the draft really began to be felt throughout the music business. Bob Crosby joined the Marines, Artie Shaw accepted a commission in the Navy, and formed a band which included his drummer, Dave Tough. Most illustrious of all those answering the call to the colours was Glenn Miller, in 1942 at the height of his fame, having just been awarded the first disc ever to be sprayed in gold paint to celebrate the millionth sale of 'Chatanooga Choo Choo'. By the end of the year there would be an all-girl band, organized by guitarist Eddie Durham, and called the Sweethearts of Rhythm, occupying the stand at the Savoy Ballroom. The new band slogan, said *Down Beat*, is 'the smaller the better'.

Moe Gale, in his wisdom, decreed that Ella should henceforth work only part of her time with the big band; for the rest of it she would be backed by an instrumental combo called the Four Keys, concentrating on club dates in the New York area, radio and recording. During such times, the band, under the direction of Eddie Barefield, would be booked as a separate unit. Which was simply another way of saying that things being how they were, the band was as good as finished. When, in August, the American Federation of Musicians ordered all of its members out of the recording studios, the old Chick Webb band just gave up the ghost.

James Caesar Petrillo of the AFM had been locked in mortal combat with the recording companies for months. He was demanding royalties on behalf of the musicians on every record made. In those days, only the artists and some of the bandleaders received a small percentage payment on the number of records sold – Petrillo saw no reason why his members too should not participate in the success generated by their work. When the record companies indignantly refused to grant his demands, Petrillo called his men out.

65

From August 1st, no musician was allowed to enter a recording studio.

The ban had some bizarre effects; the archives were raided for unreleased masters, many of them, until then, justly regarded as unreleasable. And the singers, not subject to the ban, went into the studio with vocal groups and non-union ukulele players as accompanists.

Fortunately for Ella, she landed a radio show in September. It was a sustainer, that is, a show without advertising sponsors, and it went out over the NBC Blue Network, every Monday and Wednesday night.

Down Beat's annual poll reflected what an unsatisfactory year it had been for Ella; of the first five winners, four of them were singers with the most successful of the big white bands: Helen Forrest with Harry James, Helen O'Connell with Jimmy Dorsey, Anita O'Day with Gene Krupa, and Jo Stafford with Tommy Dorsey. Billie Holiday, always too rare a taste, whose following was confined to the hard core of true jazz cognoscenti, was fourth – and Ella, almost disqualified from the category because of her work as a bandleader, could only manage thirteenth.

Duke Ellington, painting a word picture of the setting for one of his urban tone poems, wrote: 'We would like now to take you on a tour of this place called Harlem. It has always had more churches than cabarets. It is Sunday morning. We are strolling from 110th Street up Seventh Avenue, heading north through the Spanish and West Indian neighbourhood towards the 125th Street business area. Everybody is nicely dressed, and on their way to or from church. Everybody is in a friendly mood. Greetings are polite and pleasant, and on the opposite side of the street, standing under a street lamp, is a really hip chick. She, too, is in a friendly mood. You may hear a parade go by, or a funeral, or you may recognize the passage of those who are making our Civil Rights demands. (Hereabouts, in our performance, Cootie Williams pronounces the word on his trumpet – *Harlem*!)'

On Sunday, August 1st, 1943, Harlem experienced the worst riot in its history. At the Hotel Braddock on 126th Street and Eighth Avenue, an argument broke out in the lobby between the management and a black woman guest. It seems that the woman did not care for her accommodation and was demanding her money back. When the argument turned into a shouting match, a white policeman tried to arrest the woman for disturbing the peace. Joining in the fight that followed, a black soldier had snatched the policeman's nightstick, and hit him over the head with it. Whereupon the cop had shot the soldier in the shoulder and dragged him off to the nearby Sydenham Hospital, where both had their wounds attended to. A crowd gathered outside the hospital, and as the humid August evening turned into night, the rumour spread that a white policeman had shot and killed a black G.I.

By dawn of the following day, practically every shop in Harlem had had its windows smashed, cars had been overturned and set on fire, and millions of dollars' worth of merchandise had been looted. Several hundred people had been arrested, and at least six deaths had been reported.

At the height of the disturbance, the police had ordered the Savoy Ballroom to be closed, and this was regarded by many to have been a mistake. They argued that while the youth of Harlem were dancing, they would have had little time for stone throwing and shop looting. Whatever the cause of the riot, its effect was all too clear – the days of Harlem's greatness as an entertainment centre were coming to an end. By 1949, a Harlem newspaper columnist could write: 'Nobody comes to Harlem any more. Nobody seems to care ... Only a few places offer anything approaching a show, and even so it's nothing like the days when "Harlem jumped".'

One of the places that seemed unaffected by Harlem's decline was the Apollo Theatre, where Ella now frequently appeared, and where Amateur Night was still turning up some new and exciting performers. One such aspirant, early in 1943, was a toothy teenager who had accepted a dare from her friends in New Jersey. She sat at the piano and sang 'Body And Soul', and she caused a sensation. Not since Ella herself, eight years earlier, had Harlem heard anything quite so promising. Her name was Sarah Vaughan.

And it was Ella, aided and abetted by Billy Eckstine, himself an Apollo Amateur Night winner, who came rushing up to offer the newcomer such help and advice as they could. Ella warned Sarah darkly to beware of agents and managers, thus signalling that at long last, she herself was becoming aware of the shabby, off-hand way she was being treated by her own management: the bottom-of-the-barrel choice of recording titles, the gruelling hick town tours; the agency charges which reduced fees by as much as fifty per cent. In fact, she was merely voicing the preoccupation of all black artists: how do you find a manager who isn't going to rob you blind? Years later, in a radio interview, Billy Eckstine put the bitter facts: 'They'd say, you invest your talent, we'll invest our money, and we'll split fifty-fifty – after expenses. Those were the two words – "after expenses". They could write up any Goddamn thing in the world they wanted – you knew nothing about it, because you were not of their world. So after the expenses would come down, you could wind up with nothing – they would wind up with everything.'

Billy Eckstine was singing with the Earl Hines band at the time. He persuaded his boss to take Sarah Vaughan as vocalist and second pianist. By April she was playing and singing alongside Dizzy Gillespie, Charlie Parker and 'Fatha' Hines himself, and on her way to greatness.

In June, Ella appeared once more at the Apollo, and in July she opened at a new Broadway nightclub called the Zanzibar. The Zanzibar was one of those places that kept changing hands, and several promoters had come unstuck there. In its most recent manifestation it had been called the Frolic, and it was widely regarded as a 'jinxed spot'. *Down Beat* hinted darkly that 'the Street [Broadway] is going to watch Ella's venture with superstitious interest.' The rest of the show consisted of a boogie woogie pianist named Maurice Rocco – one of the first entertainers to popularize the idea of playing the piano standing up – and a big band led by Don Redman. Redman had been staff arranger for Fletcher Henderson in the twenties, and bandleader at Connie's Inn through most of the thirties. Now, at the age of forty-three, he was one of the most admired and respected musicians in the business.

The doom forecasters were confounded; the show at the Zanzibar was a triumph. The club survived, and Ella was held over for fifteen weeks.

Petrillo's recording ban was still in force, and Decca had the bright idea of teaming Ella with a vocal act which had already overtaken the Mills Brothers in popularity – the Ink Spots. They were five young men who specialized in basic

Tin Pan Alley material, and featured a lead singer named Bill Kenny, with a plaintive falsetto voice, and another who did a sort of lugubrious commentary on the text in a sepulchral baritone. They had already had enormous hits with songs like 'It's A Sin To Tell A Lie' and 'Whispering Grass', and with Ella they recorded 'Cow Cow Boogie'. The following year (1944), Ella and the Ink Spots would have a million selling hit with 'Into Each Life Some Rain Must Fall'.

> Into each life some rain must fall,
> But too much is falling in mine.

In 1945, they had another million seller, with Duke Ellington's 'I'm Beginning To See The Light'.

In October 1943, Ted Yates, of *The Age*, Harlem's local newspaper, wrote an article he called 'She Found Her Yellow Basket'. Having outlined Ella's life and career to date, he eulogized her thus: 'She did go places – clear across the country, blazing on every college campus, in every major theatre, and right to Hollywood and pictures. Ella,' he wrote, 'will always be the guileless little girl who can laugh and mean it: and cry, too. For she's real. With real ability, and with a kindness and humility she inherited from her many young years in the orphanage.'

The combination of Ella and the Ink Spots was working so well that the Gale Agency decreed another tour. This time the band was Cootie Williams'. The legendary Cootie, for eleven years heroic lead trumpet with Duke Ellington, was now another of the key members of famous orchestras who had been lured into bandleading by eager beaver managements scenting (who knows?) another Harry James or Gene Krupa bonanza.

It was a tour like all the others; full of the same frustrations and indignities. John Hammond was in the army, scouting around for talent to present at camp shows. He remembers meeting Ella and her companions in New Orleans. 'The troupe had just arrived from Atlanta, tired and unhappy with the accommodation in New Orleans. I had lunch with Ella in a miserable black hotel while she told me her troubles.'

There was worse. Don George, who wrote the lyric for Ellington's 'I'm Beginning To See The Light', was in Billy Berg's in Los Angeles, a night club noted for its gangster clientèle. He was sitting with Duke and Nat 'King' Cole – 'when a man came staggering out onstage with a knife protruding from his chest while Ella Fitzgerald was singing. Between the cigar-smoking hoods sitting at a front table, blowing smoke up in her face, and the blood-spattered man on the stage, Ella was getting much the worst of it, but great lady that she is, she stuck it out and finished the set.'

Petrillo's recording ban ended when, towards the end of the year, the manufacturers capitulated. That musicians should receive a royalty on every record they made (today a standard feature of every contract) was, in 1943, an idea so bizarre that some commentators could scarcely contain their sense of outrage. Sigmund Spaeth, in his book *A History of Popular Music in America*, called it a form of extortion, and declared that 'it was exactly the same as having a brick-layer share in the rentals of any building he helped construct, or every type-setter collect a percentage of authors' royalties and publishers' profits on every book he helped put into print.'

Successful though the strike was, it had been costly. Petrillo announced that his members had lost about seven million dollars in fees. His triumph, however, was short lived. Soon the American courts would declare the whole thing illegal, and the musicians would have to fight again a few years later.

When the musicians began recording again, Ella went back into the studios with a variety of different backings. Most congenial were the sessions with Louis Jordan and his Tympani Five. Jordan was an old Chick Webb man, so he'd known Ella from way back when she was everybody's 'Sis', sneaking off the bandstand to Lindy Hop with the customers. Since then Louis Jordan's ebullient singing style had made him famous. With the Tympani Five he'd had some really big hits: 'Knock Me A Kiss' in 1941; 'Five Guys Named Moe' in '42 – and biggest of them all, in 1944, the song he had written with his pianist Billy Austin, 'Is You Is Or Is You Ain't My Baby?' He and Ella recorded together whenever they could; that is, whenever the vagaries of touring found them both in New York at the same time. The sessions were always fun; Louis brought great humour and originality to everything he did. They sang duets together and had a great big hit with a funny West Indian calypso called 'Stone Cold Dead In De Market'.

> He's stone col' dead in de market,
> He's stone col' dead in de market,
> He's stone col' dead in de market,
> I kill nobody but me husban'.
>
> I lick him with de pot and de fryin' pan,
> I lick him with de pot and de fryin' pan,
> I lick him with de pot and de fryin' pan,
> And if I kill him – he had it comin'.

A few months later, Leonard Feather told *Melody Maker* readers how Ella, appearing at the Earth Theatre in Philadelphia 'was forced by a screaming audience to sing "Stone Cold Dead In De Market" three times before they would let her continue with her act.'

Such occasional successes notwithstanding, there were those who were deeply concerned about Ella's recording contract. One was John Hammond, who had just been asked to join the board of Keynote, a small, new recording company specializing in jazz and folk music. Among the first artists he set out to obtain for his new label was Ella Fitzgerald. 'Ella had been under contract to Decca ever since she sang 'A-Tisket, A-Tasket' with Chick Webb's band back in the 1930s, and she had not been receiving from Decca the sort of treatment I believed she deserved.'

Moe Gale asked for an annual guarantee of $40,000 for Ella, more than three times the amount she was getting from Decca. But nothing came of the deal. 'For reasons I never understood, Gale ended up by re-signing her to Decca, at the same $15,000 guarantee she had been receiving all along.'

It was another example of the way white managers betrayed their black artists: making deals behind their backs and pocketing the profits. That Decca contract was destined to last another ten years – more than twenty years over all.

The war ended, and the men who had served in the forces returned home to pick up the pieces of their professional lives. There weren't many to pick up. The big bands were sinking fast. In December 1946, eight of the biggest of them disappeared. They included Benny Goodman, Harry James, Jack Teagarden and Benny Carter. The reasons for the decline of the big bands were mainly economic: the cost of touring some seventeen to twenty musicians and singers had soared, and the big dance halls, which had flourished during the war, were now feeling the cold wind of austerity. Only the small jazz groups, nurtured by an explosion of new independent recording companies, prospered. Artie Shaw, discharged from the Navy on medical grounds, announced his intention of giving up music altogether. Later he wrote: 'The basic truth is that popular music has little or nothing to do with musical values at all. It's fundamentally functional – just one more form of "entertainment" – and the music is only incidental.'

Major Glenn Miller didn't come home at all. He was lost one terrible night in December 1944, trying to get from London to Paris in a light plane which disappeared into the English Channel. In a way, the Miller band had signalled the end of the swing band era. His bands – the civilian one, but especially his Army Air Force band, with its lush strings and its million dollars' worth of arrangements – were the ultimate in musicianly discipline and cool, calculated pro-fessionalism. But they presented no challenges. The music was no longer exciting to play. And without the excitement that the Benny Goodman men had felt when they first put up Fletcher Henderson's arrangements, it could not survive. And poor Smack was to die, broke and forgotten, in 1952.

It was perhaps typical of Dizzy Gillespie that he should have chosen such a time to form a big band. Not only a big band, but one that was to be as different from the lately departed popular favourites as Schoenberg was from Haydn. His small band records of February 1946 had caused a bigger stir in the musical world than anything since Count Basie's first big band recordings of 1937. Those four titles, 'Night In Tunisia', 'Anthropology', '52nd Street Theme', and 'Ol' Man Rebop', played by Dizzy, Milt Jackson on vibraharp, Don Byas on tenor, Al Haig, Bill DeArango and J. C. Heard on piano, guitar and drums – and a brilliant nineteen-year-old bass player named Ray Brown, had announced the ground rules for the playing of jazz from that moment on. It was no less a revolution in taste and feeling than had been the cubist discoveries of Braque and Picasso in 1907.

Just for starters, he had no money with which to buy arrangements. Instead he had to beg them and borrow them wherever he could. Billy Eckstine, whose own band was yet another casualty that year, helped out. He opened his 'book' and told Dizzy to choose whatever he wanted.

Like most musicians, Dizzy wasn't all that preoccupied with the relative merits of singers. In fact, for Gil Fuller, the composer ('One Bass Hit', 'Manteca') who had been given the job of organizing the band, this was a matter for complaint: one complaint of many. 'I also didn't like Dizzy's choice of singers. He picked a girl named Alice Roberts. I didn't think she was a real blues singer because her voice was too light.' As for Dizzy himself, he went on record in his autobiography, as follows: 'My favourites, not necessarily in this order, are Billie Holiday, Ella Fitzgerald, Sarah Vaughan, Carmen McRae and Dinah Washington. That covers everything as far as I'm concerned. Ella, I like for her impeccable tonality and her sense of rhythm.'

The new band got started at the Spotlite Club on 52nd Street, and then went on the road. Early in 1947, Dizzy booked Ella for a six week tour. 'It was a Southern tour, and

Ray Brown was in the band.... It was a really great tour, and we had a ball.' Such troubles as she'd confided to John Hammond on her last tour with Cootie and the Ink Spots were here forgotten; she loved the band, she loved Dizzy. She listened and she learned. 'That's actually the way I feel I learned how to what you call bop. It was quite an experience, and he used to always tell me, "Come on up and do it with the fellas ..." That to me was my education in learning how to really bop.'

It was only to be expected that the band would receive a mixed reception. In the smaller Southern towns, the dancers didn't know what to make of it. They stood around the bandstand and listened, trying to figure it out. The tempo was often impossibly fast, the beat obscured by Kenny Clarke's and Ray Brown's complicated embellishments. Only when a commonplace local band relieved them did the customers recognize a beat they could dance to. The process of alienation which was to separate the jazz fans from the mass audience had already begun.

James Moody, one of the sax players, describes what it was like. 'It was funny to see the reaction of the people to the band. Down there it was a little different because the people weren't quite aware of bebop, and they didn't know how to dance to the music at the time. So they would stand and look up at the band as if we were nuts, you know.' Sometimes, the atmosphere would grow distinctly hostile. 'One time, down South, this guy was looking up and he said, "Where's Ella Fitzgerald?" He was mad because he didn't see Ella Fitzgerald yet, you know. "Where's Ella Fitzgerald?" And we were playing. I think that night we kinda had to band together, to get out and leave there.'

But when they got to the big towns, they reaped their reward. In Baltimore, Washington, Chicago – the word had spread, the people came running. 'Oh, man, people, boy, they'd be wild. Lines would be all everywhere. We were playing the Paradise Theatre in Detroit. Man, the people! Just lines, crowded, coming in to see Dizzy. It was outta sight too, beautiful.'

It was the band, mostly young men, either fresh out of college or else recently demobbed (they were younger than Ella – a new experience for her), who made it such a happy tour. But mostly it was Dizzy and his wife Lorraine, one of the most devoted couples in the business, who made it so enjoyable. 'On that Southern tour,' says Ella. 'I remember that he used to always want Lorraine to make him eggs. Everywhere we'd go, he'd want Lorraine to make him eggs ... At a lotta theatres we played, my cousin and his wife used to do the cooking for everybody backstage, and everybody in the audience would be getting up because the food smell would be coming from backstage. They'd be getting the whiff. Oh, we would have some real crazy experiences, but to me it's been what you call growing up in the music, the other side of the music, and knowing that it hasn't been all easy, but worth it.'

On March 19th 1947, Ella went into the Decca Studios with an orchestra directed by Bob Haggart, lately of the Bob Crosby band, and recorded 'Lady Be Good'. It wasn't the first time she had committed her scat singing to disc: in October 1945 she had recorded 'Flying Home', an instrumental piece made famous by Benny Goodman and Lionel Hampton. But 'Lady Be Good' was important because it contained the fruits of her association with Dizzy Gillespie – it demonstrated with great clarity what she meant when she spoke of 'growing up in the music'. There was no doubt in Ella's mind that Dizzy had been 'the cause, one of the reasons I started singing "Lady Be Good". Dizzy played "Lady Be Good" with me and we jammed. He said, "Come on and risk this." To me it's been an education with Dizzy.'

Milt Gabler at Decca describes how they got it on to disc: 'When I recorded Ella's first scat things ... tape had just started to come in. And we would tape her version of it and have the arranger write stuff behind her, and she would improvise jazz licks in her interpretation of the tune

– it's her memory for jazz improvisations, her pitching and the way she swings.'

Whitney Balliet defines scat singers thus: '(They are) human horns who improvise often wordless, sometimes onomatopoeic songs, and the best of them have included Ella Fitzgerald, Anita O'Day, Jackie Cain and Roy Kral, Mel Tormé and Louis Armstrong ... But [Leo] Watson was the greatest of them all.' Leo Watson, who died in 1950, was the genius member of 'The Spirits of Rhythm', who ruled at the Onyx Club in the late thirties.

One might include in Balliet's pantheon the name of Leroy (Slam) Stewart, bass player in the double act of Slim and Slam from 1938 until 1942. He it was who invented a unique sound by bowing his double bass and singing with it an octave higher. You can hear Ella's tribute to him in part of her remarkable scat singing version of 'Lady Be Good'.

It is Louis Armstrong who is credited with having invented the form. The story goes that while recording a song called 'Heebie Jeebies' with the Hot Five in 1926, he dropped the music sheet containing the words, and had to improvise until somebody picked it up for him. Certainly we hear the now familiar 'De zat zoo zat, de zat zoo zat', followed by a growled 'an' I done forgot the words' – and so on. But then again, scat singing has always been the way jazz musicians have demonstrated musical phrases to each other when their instruments have not been readily available. Dizzy Gillespie invented 'Ooo-bop-sha-bam-a-klook-a-mop' as a way of summarizing the unique accents of bop. 'That's one of the first things I remember he would do,' says Ella. 'And "she-bop-a-da-ool-ya ... she-bop-a-da-ool-ya-coo ..." and that fascinated me. When I felt like I could sing that, then I felt like I was in, in.'

Not everybody approved of Ella's change of direction. The *Melody Maker* reviewer headlined his piece on 'Lady Be Good' – 'Ella Switches To Sweltering Swing'. 'The recipe included quotations from such songs as "Dardanella", "A-Tisket", "Yankee Doodle" and "Horses" and even grand opera. This and some of the resultant riffs and licks can hardly be described as the acme of good taste or understanding, but one readily forgives such lapses in what Ella does for the way she does it. Her astonishing control, the ease and fluency with which she puts over everything without turning a hair or bossing a note, and the terrific drive she infuses into her delivery, are things which have to be heard to be believed.'

> Oh, sweet and lovely lady be good,
> Oh, lady be good, to me.
> 'Cos I am so awfully misunderstood,
> So lady, oh lady, oh lady be good to me.

Mel Tormé, a singers' singer if ever there was one, and a fervent admirer of Ella Fitzgerald ('I don't even call her the First Lady Of Song. She is the High Priestess Of Song'), told Kitty Grime, 'The truth of the matter is that scat singing is the toughest kind of singing. There's me and Ella and Sarah and Carmen. And that's really it.' He was amazed to find that whenever Ella sang 'Lady Be Good', that it was always the same. 'She sang all the quotes on the record.' And Ella said to him, 'Mel, people have become accustomed to it.'

Bop came into its own on the night of September 29th, 1947. Billy Shaw, a booker with the Gale Agency, and a keen supporter of the new music, had said to Dizzy, 'We should have a concert with you and Ella Fitzgerald at Carnegie Hall.' Dizzy said, 'O.K., let's go.' Leonard Feather helped to promote the event. 'They did very well, surprisingly well, surprising in view of the fact that there was so much active, really nasty opposition to the music.'

The band played 'Toccata For Trumpet And Orchestra' by John Lewis, the pianist who would soon make his name with Milt Jackson, Percy Heath and Connie Kay, as the remarkable Modern Jazz Quartet. They played Dizzy's own 'Cubana Be' and 'Cubana Bop', featuring Chano Pozo, the Cuban bongo player, who, the following year, would be shot to death in a Harlem bar.

Ella sang 'Stairway To The Stars' and 'How High The Moon', and more than justified her inclusion in such company. 'After that Carnegie Hall concert,' says Dizzy, 'everybody started paying attention to the music.'

The year ended with another punch-up between Petrillo of the Musicians' Union and the record companies. This time the bone of contention was the monstrous proliferation of radio disc jockeys who were filling hours of air time with recorded music, and thus robbing the bands of live performances. This, together with the ubiquitous juke box, which was replacing musicians in bars and restaurants across the continent, called for drastic action. Petrillo announced that, after the last day of the year, there would never again be any recording of any kind, 'ever, ever, ever'. The A and R men hustled their artists into the studios in a frantic effort to beat the ban. On December 20th, Ella arrived at Decca with a pick-up band, to record her version of 'How High The Moon'.

> Somewhere there's music,
> How faint the tune,
> Somewhere there's heaven,
> How high the moon.

On that session, the bass player was the same young musician Ella had met on the Dizzy Gillespie tour – Ray Brown.

Ray Brown was born in Pittsburgh in 1926, where he studied piano and bass. He was just eighteen when he came to New York, and on the very day he arrived was introduced to Dizzy Gillespie by Hank Jones, the pianist who would later play for Ella.

'Hank said, "I want you to meet a friend of mine. This guy is a helluva bass player too." So Dizzy said, "Can you really play?" I said, "Yeah!" What the hell can you say? So he said, "You want a gig?" I said, "Yeah ...", you know.'

He was told to be at Dizzy's house for a rehearsal the following night at 1 a.m. When he got there, who does he find himself playing with but Max Roach, Bud Powell,

Dizzy Gillespie and Charlie Parker! 'Wow,' said Ray. 'Outta sight, just like that.'

Later, he was to be a member of the nascent Modern Jazz Quartet, with John Lewis, Milt Jackson and Kenny Clarke. And then Dizzy's big band of 1946.

After that, Ray and Ella began to see a lot of each other. It wasn't easy. Their work constantly found them in different cities, sometimes a thousand miles apart.

One day, Ella visited Ray in Akron, Ohio, where he was playing with a roadshow called Jazz At The Philharmonic, the brainchild of a young West Coast entrepreneur named Norman Granz.

When Ella Fitzgerald and her famous orchestra arrived in Los Angeles in 1940, a young white college boy, the same age as Ella, was waiting to greet them. Norman Granz was looking for musicians to play at the jam sessions he was running at nightclubs around the city. Visiting bands were just what he needed to fill his chairs, and L.A. in 1940 provided plenty to choose from. 'Those were good days for getting musicians in Los Angeles. Duke Ellington's band was around town; Jimmy Lunceford's men were available; Nat Cole, who had a trio at the 331 Club was my house pianist.'

With such an embarrassment of riches at his command, Granz, true jazz aficionado that he was, could take his pick. From Ella's band he chose Taft Jordan on trumpet, and Eddie Barefield on clarinet. But not Ella. She remembers it ruefully. 'Sure, he used my musicians, but he didn't want me – he just didn't dig me.' Oh yes, it's true. 'Because,' says Granz, 'in those days I didn't like Ella. I much preferred Billie Holiday.' He adds, 'And it shows how I really had an eye for good talent, d'you get me?'

Norman Granz was born on Central Avenue, in the heart of Los Angeles, in 1918. Then the family moved to Long Beach, California, where his father owned a department store, and where, says Granz, 'we were one of about half a dozen Jewish families in the whole city.'

The Depression brought hard times, the store was lost, and their reduced circumstances forced the family to move to the district known as Boyle Heights in Los Angeles. There he graduated from Roosevelt High School in 1935, then took a job in order to work his way through college.

It was while he was at UCLA, that he conceived the idea of staging jam sessions. He was not a musician himself, but he loved the company of musicians, imitating their mannerisms and modes of speech. He made a friend of Lee Young, brother of Lester, the famed 'Prez', and Nat 'King' Cole (then just a good jazz pianist who didn't sing) remembered him as this kid who bought all the new records, and would bring them around to the house for Nat and his friends to listen to and discuss. 'I suppose,' says Granz, 'that the reason I can mix so easily with minority members arose from my playing with the kids on Central Avenue, when it was a heterogeneous district with all minorities represented.'

Granz knew that jazz musicians enjoyed sitting down together to make music of their own choosing, a relaxation for which they never got paid. He also sensed that there was an audience for it – not a dancing crowd, but a *listening* one; lovers of the music who would simply sit and listen to it, appreciating the skill and artistry that went into its making, the way other people attended a classical music concert.

He went to the nightclub owner Billy Berg (that same Billy Berg in whose club Ella had shared the stage with a wounded gangster), and proposed that he run jam sessions one night every week. This was possible because the AF of M had recently guaranteed the regular musicians in such places, one night off in every seven.

He paid his chosen musicians $6 a night, take it or leave it, and filled the dance floor with tables and chairs. These sessions were to be miniature concerts and to hell with the jitterbugs. But by far the most important rule was: Negro patrons were to be made welcome – something never before permitted in a Hollywood nightclub.

On the twenty-fifth anniversary of his Jazz At The Philharmonic, Norman Granz spoke to Derek Jewell of the *Sunday Times* about those days: 'Billie Holiday came crying to me – because her friends couldn't go into this club in Los Angeles to hear her. So I went to the owner and said why didn't he let me take over the place on the day he was closed

82

and run a jam session. I did it and I completely desegregated the house. I had Nat Cole's trio and Lester Young and some of Duke's musicians. It was very successful and the club owner didn't worry about black and white once he saw the green.' It was to become the guiding principle behind all his subsequent promotions.

Norman Granz had gone into the army in 1941. Invalided out in 1943, he had gone to work at Warner Brothers film studio as a labourer, then at MGM as a film editor. In 1944, in order to help a defence fund for some Mexican boys who had been sent to prison after a murder trial which had reeked of prejudice, Granz decided to stage a concert with his jamming musicians. 'The big auditorium in L.A. is the Philharmonic. I designed a bill which said "Jazz Concert At The Philharmonic", but it wouldn't fit the type-size I wanted. So I dropped the word "concert". That's how the title happened.'

His cast included Les Paul, not exactly a jazz guitarist, but one of the first to exploit the resources of the electrically amplified instrument, and make a fortune from it; Meade Lux Lewis, the boogie-woogie pianist who had been famous in 1929 for his recording of 'Honky Tonk Train Blues', had dropped out of sight for several years and had then been tracked down by John Hammond who found him washing cars in a Chicago garage, and a tenor player named Illinois Jacquet, whose screaming high notes could trigger off an almost frenzied response in his young audience. The concert was such a success that as a result Granz was able to present a concert at the Philharmonic every month.

The following year, Granz teamed up with a Chicago booker named Berle Adams (he later became a big noise with M.C.A., the Music Corporation of America), and together they planned to take Jazz At The Philharmonic on tour. The idea was to form a group of some half a dozen or so big jazz names, plus a girl singer – Helen Humes, lately with Count Basie, was the first choice – and to add local talent in all the cities visited.

The first tour was a dismal failure. They worked their way

up the West Coast, but by the time they had reached Canada, audiences were so sparse that the whole enterprise collapsed. By the time Granz was ready to try again, he had released several records, captured live at the concerts (another Granz innovation), and with Lester Young and Coleman Hawkins among the group, the show was a hit. Says Granz: 'For the next eleven years we did two ten-week tours a year, covering about fifty or sixty towns each time. We never played a segregated concert – not even in New Orleans.'

There were differences of opinion about the music played at JATP concerts. Some said it was flashy, and deliberately crowd pleasing; one bone of contention was Granz's predilection for 'battles'. 'Norman had a weird sense of competition,' wrote Dizzy Gillespie of a later tour. 'JATP wasn't much musically because Norman Granz got his nuts off by sending two or three trumpet players out there to battle one another's brains out on the stage. And he'd just sit back and laugh. He'd get Flip Phillips, Illinois Jacquet and Lester Young, then have Roy Eldridge and me as the two trumpet players.... and then they'd have a drum battle with Buddy Rich and Louis Bellson. It was funny, battling all the time.'

Be that as it may, the musicians were more than content. There they were, playing the music they loved, of which they were the masters, and getting handsomely paid for it too. But especially, they appreciated the treatment they received on tour. It was first class. Wrote Dizzy: 'You travelled "first class", stayed in "first class" hotels.'

It is impossible to overstress what this must have meant to the black musicians, all of whose experience had been precisely the opposite. In a way, the handful of singers and instrumentalists who had begun to work with white bands had suffered most bitterly in this regard, perhaps because of the manifest contrast between their treatment and that of their white confrères. Writing about Lena Horne's tour with the Charlie Barnet band in 1939, Jim Haskins wrote: 'There were places the band appeared where Lena was accepted as a performer but not as an onlooker – it was okay for her to get up on the stage and sing, but when the song was over she couldn't sit on stage between numbers with the musicians. This was unacceptable racial mixing.' When she was refused a room at the band's hotel, Charlie Barnet would cancel the reservation and search for a hotel that would take the entire ensemble.

When Billie Holiday was singing with Artie Shaw at the Lincoln Hotel in New York, the management made her enter and leave the hotel through the kitchens, and use the freight elevator to get from ballroom to bandroom. But the saddest story of all, again concerning Artie Shaw, was that told by Roy Eldridge to *Down Beat*, about the time when he was featured trumpet player with that band. 'I went to a place where we were supposed to play a dance, and they wouldn't even let me in the place. "This is a white dance," they said, and there was my name right outside, Roy 'Little Jazz' Eldridge, and I told them who I was. When finally I did get in, I played that first set, trying to keep from crying. By the time I got through the set, the tears were rolling down my cheeks. I don't know how I made it. I went to the dressing room and stood in a corner crying and saying to myself, "Why the hell did I come out here again when I knew what would happen?" Artie came in and he was real great. He made the guy apologize to me that wouldn't let me come in and got him fired. Man, when you're on the stage, you're great, but as soon as you come off, you're nothing. It's not worth the glory, not worth the money, not worth anything.'

Norman Granz comments on his policy like this: 'I felt that it made no kind of sense to treat a musician with any kind of respect and dignity onstage and then make him go around to the back door when he's offstage. I don't understand that treatment. So wherever we went, we stayed in the best hotels. We travelled the best way because I think that's all part of it. Because it didn't make sense for me to get a cat to work for me at Carnegie Hall, and then after work, he goes to the Alvin Hotel. That doesn't make sense. He's supposed to be treated as a great artist on and off the stage.

It wasn't only antiblack discrimination, it was discrimination against musicians. ... I don't mean to be dramatic, but I insisted that my musicians were to be treated with the same respect as Leonard Bernstein or Heifetz because they were just as good, both as men and musicians. It took a long time to convince the concert halls, even though I was paying the rent. Pretty hard to get away from those prejudices.'

Ray Brown was the bass player on those early JATP tours, and he and Ella were thinking seriously about getting married. Ella paid one of her visits to Ray when the show was in Akron, Ohio. Seated out front for the performance, she was quickly recognized by the audience, who insisted that she get up there on the stage and give them a song. Norman Granz rather reluctantly consented to allow it (Helen Humes was his singer with the show), and by the time Ella had finished her song, and received an ovation for it, Granz had changed his mind about her: 'I felt that it made sense to have her work with the group, particularly considering her liaison with Ray Brown.'

There and then he offered her a contract, and Ella was happy to accept it. It may indeed have helped Ray and Ella come to a decision about their private lives, for very soon after they were married.

Ella, however, was not free to start work with JATP right away. There were dates, already booked, which had to be fulfilled. Petrillo's recording ban was still in force, the big bands had all but disappeared, the 52nd Street clubs were closing, and managements were beginning to look beyond the shores of the United States for new markets. The Atlantic beckoned. Great Britain and the continent of Europe, shaking themselves into life after six years of war, were clamouring for the chance to see and hear the stars they knew only from radio, records and the movies. In 1947, Broadway had already enchanted London with Rodgers and Hammerstein's *Oklahoma!* and Irving Berlin's *Annie Get Your Gun*, and that summer, an unknown entertainer named

Danny Kaye would so delight the audience at the London Palladium, that it seemed they would never let him go. It was time for jazz to make the crossing.

In January 1948, Dizzy Gillespie sailed for Sweden with a big band. They were greeted like the messengers of light. Later Dizzy wrote: 'All over that small country the Swedes really dug the music. Denmark was the greatest.' In Paris they played three completely sold out concerts. 'We had Paris jumping too,' wrote Dizzy. 'Just like Harlem.'

Ray Brown was asked to go on that tour, but decided to decline the offer. 'I'd just gotten married to Ella Fitzgerald. At the time I was in a bit of a curl between her wanting me to travel with her as well. She wanted me to travel with the trio; she had Hank Jones playing piano. So finally I just decided that I was gonna stay in New York.'

He did, but not for long. By the summer, Ella had accepted an offer to visit England.

In July, *Melody Maker* breathlessly announced the coming event: 'Swing enthusiasts will be thrilled to learn that Ella Fitzgerald – America's "First Lady Of Song" – is the latest addition to the U.S. personality parade visiting Britain this year ... Although Ella has long been eminent in the field of swing singing, there is no doubt that she now stands at the zenith of her career. Today she is generally accepted by musicians and fans alike as one of the outstanding singers in jazz.'

On September 15th, the newly wed Mr and Mrs Brown arrived in Southampton on the *Queen Mary*. Ella was scheduled to open at the London Palladium on the 27th, but Betty Hutton (billed as the Platinum Screwball), whose engagement preceded hers, had been such a success that the management had persuaded Ella to begin her tour in Scotland, at the Empire Theatre in Glasgow.

English musicians had long known that theatre, then exclusively a vaudeville house, to be a safe haven for their music; the audience were warm, appreciative and knowledgeable, especially receptive to visiting Americans. In contrast, English variety artists, crossing the border into Scotland (in particular, English comedians), were often greeted as unwelcome foreigners; the date had become known as 'the comics' graveyard'. Vaudeville, or Variety, shows were given twice nightly, usually with matinées on Wednesday and Saturday – a total of fourteen performances a week.

Ella appeared on the Monday in front of a packed house, and nursing a bad head cold. Observers noted that she seemed nervous. But since Norman Granz says he has never seen her do a show when she *wasn't* nervous, this must be taken as having been nothing unusual. Accompanied onstage by Hank Jones, a fine pianist with great delicacy of touch, and the estimable Ray Brown, she opened with 'Cow Cow Boogie', followed that with a ballad, 'Don't Worry 'Bout Me', and then an exuberant version of 'The Woody Woodpecker Song'. She went on to sing 'Nature Boy', the song that had been such an enormous hit for Nat 'King' Cole – and finished with the inevitable 'A-Tisket, A-Tasket'. A storm of applause brought her back onstage, and Ella was startled to hear the audience calling for requests, the most insistent being for 'My Happiness'. This song, recorded by Ella during the recording ban with a vocal act called the Song Spinners, had been a considerable hit in the States, but Ella was quite unprepared to find that the record was well known in Britain, three thousand miles from New York. She struggled her way through it, but the next day she had to go out and buy a copy of the record in order to familiarize herself with the arrangement.

The following week she opened at the London Palladium. There, because the Palladium was the most important Variety theatre in Europe, she was not 'top of the bill'. That position was occupied by the nation's most beloved entertainer, Gracie Fields. The audience was appreciative, but *Melody Maker* had some reservations: 'We who know her voice so well and admire it so much felt, however, that for some reason, we were not seeing Ella at her best. Although

Ella and Oscar

Ella and Frank Sinatra in 1969. 'Frank always sends me yellow roses'

Ella: 'I love ballads'

Maternal Ella: 'I love
babies'

It's Jazz at the Philharmonic time. Ella with Stan Getz

71. Ella with two of her favourite
en, Louis Armstrong and Duke
lington. The occasion is an awards
remony in Las Vegas

A distinguished trio: Princess Margaret, Duke Ellington and Ella

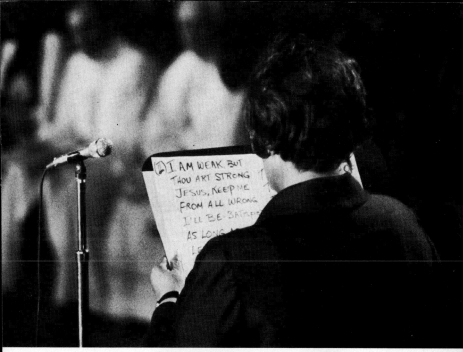

At Duke Ellington's funeral
n 1974. Ella's eyes are
eginning to trouble her

Ella arrives in London in
1980, her first visit in three
years

Ella Fitzgerald, the lady alone with her music

she sang as impeccably as ever, with style and phrasing that are unsurpassed, she seemed to lack stage personality, and was obviously labouring under great nervous tension at the opening show on Monday night.'

That remark about her lack of stage personality may have been a typically British reaction, polite and euphemistic, to seeing for the first time, in the flesh, the 'skinny kid' (Ella's own description of herself) who had won their hearts with 'A-Tisket' and 'Mr Paganini' back in the thirties. Ever since her film appearance in *Ride 'Em Cowboy*, Ella had been putting on weight in quite an alarming fashion. Now, at the age of thirty, she must have appeared almost matronly. To the British, who were wont to think of American entertainers as resembling the frenetic Betty Hutton, it must have come as a profound shock. In many ways it must have been a cruel ordeal, in those days before her audience had completely accepted her, for Ella to appear in public at all.

The audience at the Palladium had not been drawn there by Ella's presence on the bill; they had come for the most part to see Gracie Fields – 'Our Gracie' as they called her – in one of her rare appearances in her native land. Warmly welcoming though they were, the American singer was a mere added attraction. But Ella had the chance to meet her real admirers, the night after the Palladium engagement ended. This was at a Sunday concert featuring Ted Heath and his music, at the same theatre. Ted Heath, a trombone player of some note, had put together a late-flowering swing band which was good enough to stand comparison with the best of America's swing era. A musicianly, hard driving outfit, it would be the last of Britain's big bands to survive.

When Ella walked on stage with Ray Brown and Hank Jones, she heard a sound which almost bowled her over. *Melody Maker* reported: 'The ear-splitting ovation given to guest singer Ella Fitzgerald at Ted Heath's London Palladium Swing Session last Sunday, far surpassed that accorded any swing artist appearing on the British stage since the war.' Ella stood there, amazed. She simply couldn't believe it. But then, Ella never did. As Leonard

89

Feather told *Playboy* magazine in 1957: 'Ella Fitzgerald has never fully recognized the extent of her fame or talent; she is constantly amazed at her reputation.'

She sang 'How High The Moon', 'Lady Be Good', and 'Flying Home', and the audience clamoured for more. Said *Melody Maker*: 'Again and again she was recalled by the bop-hungry semi-hysterical crowd who seemed determined to keep America's "First Lady of Song" on the stage until midnight.' Ray Brown took the band through his Dizzy Gillespie number, 'Big Bass Hit'; Ella forgot her nervousness and had a ball. She jived in front of Ted Heath's men and was genuinely impressed by the way they played. Before leaving New York, she had met and heard the British pianist George Shearing, who had settled in America. She told an English reporter, 'If George is anything to go by, then I just can't believe – as I've sometimes heard – that you're lacking in swing ability over here.'

Ella had enjoyed her first brief visit to Europe. The British people had been warm and welcoming; in spite of the fact that food rationing was still in force, she had eaten well, and there had been a decent place to stay. She would not have noticed that it was still impossible for her and her husband to have checked in at any of London's 'first class' hotels. (Things had, however, improved since the war. When, in 1932, Louis Armstrong had arrived in England, his sponsors had telephoned a dozen hotels before finding one which would take him in.) On October 30th, Ella, together with Ray Brown and Hank Jones, boarded the *Queen Elizabeth* and sailed for home. She could have had no idea how much a part of her life foreign travel would soon become.

Television in America was extending its range and power. By 1949, with New York, Washington, Boston, Chicago and St Louis joined together by coaxial cable, the first signs of a coast-to-coast national network were to be seen. But so far, nobody in TV had succeeded in doing anything much about music, either classical or popular. There was a *New Yorker* cartoon at the time, which depicted a couple watching a symphony concert on their set. One is saying to the other: 'It's even better if you shut your eyes.'

However, Esmé Sarnoff, who was married to Robert Sarnoff, son of General Sarnoff, the chairman of RCA, had managed, against all the odds, to get a jazz show on the air. 'Somehow,' wrote John Hammond (he was later to marry Esmé), 'she had persuaded the general to allow her to produce a jazz television show for NBC, a remarkable feat for the daughter-in-law of the boss.' The show was hosted by that stalwart champion of Dixieland jazz, Eddie Condon, and featured people like Louis Armstrong and a lot of other big time musicians. It was also the show on which Ella got her first chance to appear on the magic box.

Her recordings in the first half of that year were the usual Decca gallimaufry of awful songs and indifferent accompaniments. Apart from a nice 'Baby, It's Cold Outside' with Louis Jordan, everything else she did is totally forgettable. It was all the more frustrating for her, since Columbia records had just introduced the most significant advance in recording technology since the electromechanized system of two decades earlier – the long-playing record. Now that twenty minutes and more of music could be captured on each side of a twelve-inch disc, the entire future of recording was about to be transformed. Together with the other recently new facility of recording on magnetic tape, it meant that, for the first time, improvising virtuosi like Coleman Hawkins, Roy Eldridge and Charlie Parker were no longer cramped within the confines of a three-minute, ten-inch disc format, but could spread themselves as freely as they habitually did whenever they sat in and jammed in a night club. Or, come to that, whenever they played onstage in Jazz At The Philharmonic.

New ideas are often the result of the confluence between a technological advance and a subjective need (witness how powerful amplification and the Beatles seemed to arrive on the scene together), and Norman Granz had grasped the opportunity to record his virtuoso soloists on the new format. He set about recording all his concerts, live, in their place of origin, editing them and issuing them as long-playing records. Between 1948 and 1951, the records appeared on the Mercury label; but in that year, Granz recalled the rights to all his own recordings and reissued them under his own label, which he called Clef.

When Ella Fitzgerald began touring with Jazz At The Philharmonic in 1948, the most painful piece of editing Norman Granz had to do was to excise Ella herself. Because of her long-standing contract with Decca, everything she did at the concerts had to be cut out off the records. It made Granz extremely angry, and he began to figure out a way to change the situation. He was already convinced that the Gale Agency, Moe Gale and his brother Tim, had been handling Ella all those years without the respect due to an artist of her rare talents, and that Milt Gabler at Decca had offered her material to record which was often contemptible and frequently insulting.

Ella was perfectly aware that all was not well; she would often object to Decca's choice of songs for her; but such was her temperament and training, that, as Tim Gale remembers, 'She would sing *anything* if her advisers insisted.' (One could paraphrase the old witticism thus: 'With advisors like that, who needs dictators!') Tim Gale recalls: 'One of her records was a thing called "My Happiness". She cut it under protest; I brought the dub backstage to her at the Paramount, and she said, "It's a shame. A corny performance of a corny song." It turned out to be one of her biggest sellers.'

Big seller or not, Granz was certain that the kind of manipulative treatment that produced such hits was utterly wrong. 'I was adamant that she be given the right to do what she wanted.' What Ella wanted to do was ballads. Ballads were what she wanted to sing. She'd been, she freely confessed, a frustrated ballad singer from way back when. Leonard Feather reports that 'she once burst into tears when Chick Webb ("He didn't think I was ready to sing ballads") assigned to the band's male vocalist a tune that had been specially arranged for Ella.' Very well then. 'Ballads,' decreed Norman Granz, 'is what, in my shows, she is going to sing.'

But that, he discovered, presented a whole new set of problems. What would happen was this: Ella would start on something slow and soulful, something by the Gershwins or Rodgers and Hart, and she would have scarcely got past the fourth bar, before some kid at the back would yell out 'How High The Moon' or 'Lady Be Good'. Ella, the quintessentially nervous performer, would hesitate, stop singing, and then, with a panic-stricken glance at her accompanist, launch herself into the requested song. 'We finally worked a gimmick up,' says Granz. 'We'd do not only *a* ballad, we'd do two in a row. And that finally forced the public to mind its manners.'

Ella was happy singing her ballads. She was also, Granz discovered, the most bountiful of performers. 'I'll say I want her to sing eight tunes, and she'll say, "Don't you think that's too many? Let's make it six." And she'll go out there and do six, and then if the audience wants fifty, she'll stay for forty-four more. It's part of her whole approach to life. She just loves to sing.'

Granz had come a long way from preferring other singers. In 1952, he was able to say to a reporter from London's *New Musical Express*: 'Ella Fitzgerald reigns today, unchallenged, as the champion girl singer of our time.'

In 1949, Mr and Mrs Ray Brown moved into a house in St Albans in the borough of Queens, just across the East River from Harlem, and Ella began to think about creating a family. Her own years in the orphanage had led her, inevitably, to take an interest in the fate of other children, similarly deprived, and in 1945, she had been elected to the International Committee of the Foster Parents' Plan for World Children (among her fellow committee members were Mrs Harry Truman and Mrs Eleanor Roosevelt).

Ray and Ella decided to adopt a baby boy and call him Raymond Brown Junior. When their marriage broke up three years later, Ray Junior continued to live with Ella and he grew to manhood in her care.

Meanwhile, their professional life went on. Ray and Ella worked together on the JATP tours, and got back to Queens and Raymond Junior whenever they got the chance.

By 1950, Decca, along with the rest of the record business, had caught up with Columbia and jumped eagerly aboard the LP bandwagon. Ella's first foray into this exciting new world was a modest enough enterprise, but it was one which would presage important events still to come. In September, she went into the studio with a pianist named Ellis Larkins, to record an album of George Gershwin songs. They worked for two days, and recorded fourteen songs. Milt Gabler chose eight of them to release as a ten-inch album called *Ella Sings Gershwin*. Later, when ten-inch LP's had lost their appeal, he added a few more tracks and reissued it as a twelve-inch album.

She enjoyed herself enormously. She responded avidly to the quality of the material, and why not? Her last recording for Milt Gabler had been 'Santa Claus Got Stuck In My Chimney'(!). Her favourite songs were 'My One And Only', 'Nice Work If You Can Get It', and 'Someone To Watch Over Me'. Especially she appreciated, for the first time, being able to sing the verses, those *colla voce* introductory explorations of the theme of the song, of which Ira Gershwin was the master. Verses were an essential part of the musical theatre songs of the twenties and thirties, but band vocalists like Ella Fitzgerald were chorus singers (stand up, sing a chorus, sit down). Discovering songs which were more than thirty-two bars long came as a delightful surprise. This is the verse that Ira Gershwin wrote for 'Someone To Watch Over Me', for the musical comedy *Oh, Kay!*, in 1926.

94

There's a saying old,
Says that love is blind,
Still we're often told,
Seek and ye shall find;
So I'm going to seek a certain lad
I've had
In mind.
Looking ev'rywhere,
Haven't found him yet,
He's a big affair
I can not forget;
Only man I ever think of
With regret.
I'd like to add his initials to my monogram,
Tell me, where is the shepherd
For this lost lamb...

Ellis Larkins, a pianist who has been described as the Gerald Moore of jazz – in other words, the perfect vocal accompanist – remembers Ella's dazzling skills; her quick comprehension of the essence of a song, and her mastery of its lyrical nuances; her ability, once having mastered a routine, to repeat it immediately and impeccably; her incredible memory for lyrics. Ella returned the compliment. 'Ellis Larkins doesn't do much talking. He does most of his talking with his fingers. He just seems to have an ear for what a singer can do, and it's easy working with him.'

But then, Ella has always been lucky with her accompanists. Or possibly it's because she draws the best of them to her. There was Hank Jones, and later there would be Jimmy Rowles and Tommy Flanagan and Don Abney. And waiting in the wings was the man who was destined to play a more important part in her life than any other musician.

Oscar Peterson was born in Montreal in 1925. He was enjoying a big local reputation, and resisting all efforts to lure him to New York (Jimmy Lunceford had tried and failed), when Norman Granz heard him play at the Alberta Lounge in Montreal, and made him an offer he simply couldn't refuse – a concert with Jazz At The Philharmonic at Carnegie Hall. Oscar is a genial giant of a man, with a piano style which reminds many of the great Art Tatum, a not-so-surprising fact, as Oscar will freely admit that his discovery of Tatum completely changed his life. It will suffice here to say that his impact on the world of jazz was such that he won the *Down Beat* piano award every year from 1950 to 1955.

Almost as soon as he had joined the JATP entourage, Oscar met Ray Brown, and together with guitarist Irving Ashby, they formed the Oscar Peterson Trio. That trio was to become an integral part of Ella Fitzgerald's work for many years to come.

Irving Ashby, the guitarist, soon made way for Barney Kessel and then Herb Ellis, but Ray Brown stayed with Oscar for all the years he was with Granz. Both he and Oscar were deeply serious musicians who worked at refining their playing whenever they had the chance. Ben Webster, the ex-Ellington tenor player, remembers: 'I never saw anyone as keen on music as Oscar and Ray. They were always working on something or going over something to make it better. I remember being on a JATP tour with them, and at every concert, when the curtains went down for the interval, they'd be there right behind the curtain, right through till the concert began again. They'd be at it before the concert and after it as well.'

The result was a degree of musical rapport which bordered on the uncanny. Says Ray Brown: '. . . Oscar wrote some hard music, but he didn't write it down. We had to memorize all of it . . . And Oscar would play a tune in one key one night and walk in and play the whole arrangement in another key a week later.' And Ella reaped the benefit of all that hard work. She couldn't have been happier, and Oscar declared that of all the singers he had accompanied, Ella was his 'utmost favourite': 'It is such a joy to play for Ella.'

In 1952, Norman Granz and Jazz At The Philharmonic took off for Europe. The tour was to take them to fourteen countries. They were a formidable group: Roy Eldridge and Charlie Shavers on trumpets, Lester Young and Flip Phillips on tenors; two drummers, Buddy Rich and Gene Krupa; the Oscar Peterson Trio, Oscar, Ray, and Barney Kessel on guitar – and Ella.

Barney Kessel, a marvellous musician from Oklahoma, who had worked with Charlie Barnet and Artie Shaw, was fascinated by Ella, and the way singing seemed to be her whole life. He told Kitty Grime: 'I remember once in Genoa, Italy, we sat down to eat and the restaurant was empty except for Lester Young and his wife and Ella and me. So while we waited to give our breakfast order, I pulled out my guitar and she and Lester started making up fabulous things on the blues. Another time, when we were touring Switzerland, instead of gossiping with the rest of the troupe on the bus, she and I would get together and she'd take some tune like "Blue Lou" and sing it every way in the world. She would try to exhaust every possibility, as if she was trying to develop improvisation to a new point by ad-libbing lyrically too, the way calypso singers do.'

Ella's contribution to the show was a set accompanied by the Oscar Peterson Trio – a combination of talents which was to make music together for the next quarter of a century, delighting audiences all over the world, and recording dozens of albums. With her husband by her side, Ella should have been blissfully happy, but alas, by the time the company returned to New York, the marriage was over.

The bi-annual tours continued, and his break-up with Ella did not prevent Ray Brown from once again joining JATP for another whirl around, early in 1953. This time the personnel was Lester Young and Flip Phillips on tenor saxes, Willie Smith on alto, Charlie Shavers on trumpet, Gene Krupa and J. C. Heard on drums, the Oscar Peterson Trio, and Ella.

And this time, the British Musicians' Union granted them permission to visit England. The M.U., reacting to the

A.F. of M.'s refusal to allow British musicians to work in America, had retaliated by banning American musicians from Britain. Norman Granz had asked to be allowed to play two charity concerts in aid of the disastrous floods which had devastated parts of North Devon earlier in the year. The Musicians' Union could hardly refuse, and Jazz At The Philharmonic became the first American jazz group to play in England for sixteen years. The concerts, in March 1953, were at the Gaumont State in London, one of those barn-like super-cinemas of the 30s which has long since closed its doors. Ella scored a tremendous personal success, but, true to her own demanding standards, she was far from satisfied. Mike Butcher of the *New Musical Express* reported that 'she was almost in tears backstage because she thought she had sung so badly. This, despite the fact that the crowd had cheered her to the echo!'

That year, Ella at last won over the critics. *Down Beat* conducted, for the first time, a poll with a difference. This was to be a Critics' Poll – in other words, the jury were those who considered themselves to be the true cognoscenti. Among the girl singers, Ella came first, and second place was a tie between Billie Holiday and Sarah Vaughan.

On a plane which was taking the Jazz At The Philharmonic company from Tokyo to Osaka, Norman Granz at last raised a subject which had been on his mind for a couple of years. 'I had become convinced, not that I could be the best manager for Ella Fitzgerald, but certainly that I could be better than the manager she had at the time.' For Granz, a man not given to dissimulation, this was a massive understatement. Ella's personal management was still, after all these years, in the hands of the Gale Agency; but there was now somebody else in the picture – it was the toughest agent in the business, Joe Glaser.

According to James Lincoln Collier, in his biography of Louis Armstrong: 'Joe Glaser chose to live his life as if he were a character from a Damon Runyon story: the Broadway sharp with gangland connections, who knew where the bodies had been dumped, could pull strings at City Hall, but had, nonetheless, a heart of gold. At least that was the way he was seen by the people he did business with.' In 1935, down on his luck, Glaser had spotted an opening representing black artists – something not many white agents were prepared to do. He took over Louis Armstrong's management, and boasted, 'I'm going to control everything in black show business before I'm through.' He soon had on his books Andy Kirk, Billie Holiday, Sarah Vaughan, Pearl Bailey and many more.

In the forties, he merged his company, the Associated Booking Corporation, with the Gale Agency, and thus did Ella come under his control. Glaser had the usual rough-hewn, avuncular attitude towards his black clients that was the orthodoxy of the times; immensely talented they might be, but they were just a bunch of unruly, sometimes wayward children all the same; and like children, they were certainly not to be trusted with too much money.

Granz put his case to Ella. He told her that her whole career seemed to him aimless, particularly with regard to her recordings. He conceded that her records sold well, but that, nonetheless, she was singing the wrong kind of songs, and that she had too little control over their choice. Ella was afraid at first. 'She thought I was too much of a blowtop,' says Granz. 'So I told her it was a matter of pride with me, that she still hadn't been recognized – economically at least – as the greatest singer of our time.'

The economic strand of the argument was almost too obvious to need re-stating. It was common knowledge that Joe Glaser took 50% of Louis Armstrong's earnings, and Irving Mills had a similar arrangement with Duke Ellington. Billy Eckstine said in a radio interview: '[Ella] was supposed to be the first lady of song, and she's getting the *seventy-fifth* lady of song's money, you know?'

Granz asked Ella to give him a year's free trial, he would take no commission. Ella agreed. With the proviso that she paid her commission just like everybody else. And so, in 1954, Norman Granz became Ella's personal manager. 'We both agreed at the time that we had no contract, so each could have the luxury of leaving the other if it didn't work.'

The improvement in Ella's fortunes was immediate and spectacular. Besides the bi-annual JATP tours, Granz began getting her into the better sort of clubs, places she had never played. Not only that, but she began to earn the kind of money she was really worth, and it was a great deal.

Ever since Benny Goodman's first concert at Carnegie in 1938, and John Hammond's 'From Spirituals To Swing' concerts that same year, the idea that an audience might be attracted to listen to jazz rather than dance to it no longer seemed as outlandish as once it did. And now, with JATP regularly appearing at Carnegie Hall and on tour, the jazz concert, as a concept, was firmly established. The next, inevitable step along the road to complete respectability was the Jazz Festival.

In 1954, Louis Lorillard, heir to a tobacco fortune, and his wife Elaine, decided to organize such a festival in their home town of Newport, Rhode Island. To help organize it they recruited George Wein, a young pianist from Boston, just setting himself up as an impresario, and Professor Marshall Stearns of Hunter College, where he had founded an Institute of Jazz Studies. And they invited John Hammond to be a member of their advisory committee. Hammond was dubious. He knew Newport, some of his family lived there; it was the richest and most exclusive enclave in the land, and he questioned whether the residents would take kindly to a sudden invasion by large numbers of black musicians, making loud and, to Newportian ears, rude noises. 'I'd be happy to be associated with such a festival,' he said. 'But accommodations for Negro artists and Negro patrons would have to be arranged first.'

The Lorillards were undeterred. The necessary arrangements were made, and the Festival, in the grounds of the Newport Casino, went ahead. 'As I expected,' wrote John Hammond, 'the town split pro and con over the influx of musicians and jazz fans, and old residents were startled by the number of photographers and reporters who arrived from everywhere for this incredible story of an explosion of jazz in the sacred precincts. We also had bad luck with the weather, which was stinko.'

Stan Kenton was the Master of Ceremonies, and over the two days of the festival, an audience of some 10,000 listened to Dizzy Gillespie, Eddie Condon and a Chicago-style group, the Oscar Peterson Trio (with Barney Kessel and Ray Brown), and Ella Fitzgerald. A good time was had by all; all, that is, except the board of the snooty Newport Casino, who were dismayed to find that the chairs, aided and abetted by the rain, had churned up their lovingly tended tennis courts into a viscous bog.

On the other hand the Lorillards were delighted (the

Festival even made a small profit), and George Wein went on to produce Newport Jazz Festivals annually until 1959, then similar events in French Lick, Indiana, Toronto and Boston.

Musical battles were not the only kind that Norman Granz seemed to enjoy. As JATP progressed across America and around the world, he was constantly scrapping with one authority or another in his never-ending war on behalf of his musicians and their inalienable rights. A lot of his time was spent in what he called 'breaking down hotels' – persuading them, often bullying them into accepting his black musicians as guests. It became something of an obsession. As Ray Brown remembers: 'That was as important to him as the concert. We used to plan our strategy on the airplanes. He'd wire all these big hotels and send two or three of us to each one.' If the hotels resisted, Granz would blow his top and threaten to sue everybody in sight.

As long ago as 1947, in Jackson, Michigan, Granz and his men had staged the first lunch counter sitdown (like the bus boycott, the lunch counter sitdown was to become a favourite tactic for Civil Rights activists all over America). The musicians waited behind each counter stool, ready to sit in it as soon as it was vacated. Says Granz: 'We were half an hour late for the concert, and we still hadn't eaten – but we made our point.'

On July 20th, 1954, Ella Fitzgerald, John Lewis, her pianist on that tour, and Georgianna Henry, Ella's cousin by marriage, who accompanied her as maid, dresser and companion, flew into Honolulu airport, a scheduled stop-over on the route to Australia. As always, they all held first-class tickets, booked and verified weeks in advance. They left the plane to rendezvous with Norman Granz, who would then fly on with them to Sydney. When all four returned to the plane, they were told that their first-class tickets were not valid, and that they would have to sit in the second-class section. Granz was enraged, but mindful of the fact that they had dates to fulfil, he offered a compromise: Ella would travel first-class, while he, John and Georgianna would travel second. This suggestion was turned down; not only that, but Ella was not even allowed back into first in order to collect her personal luggage – a steward was sent in to bring it out. Whereupon Norman Granz refused to travel at all. As a result, the party spent three frustrating days in Honolulu waiting for a connecting flight to Sydney, and completely missed some of their engagements.

In January 1955, Norman Granz sued Pan American World Airways for $270,000. The suit charged Pan Am with violating the Civil Aeronautics Act, which prohibits prejudice and discrimination against passengers.

The music went on. But so did the battles. On the next tour, Dizzy Gillespie joined them. There was also Lester Young, Flip Phillips and Illinois Jacquet on tenors; Roy Eldridge on trumpet, the Oscar Peterson Trio, which now included the great guitarist Herb Ellis; Buddy Rich on drums – and Ella. This time they penetrated deeper into the South than ever before, and, as usual, Granz had chartered a private plane so that the company need not spend the night in any town that might prove hostile.

In Charleston, South Carolina, there was trouble because the proprietor of the concert hall had apparently violated some City Ordinance which prohibited mixed audiences. The situation was fraught with danger, and Georgianna Henry was persuaded to stuff the night's takings down the front of her dress and sneak off with them to the waiting plane. The rest of the company followed later, and when all were safely on board, they zoomed off into the night.

On that same tour, for the first time, JATP played Houston, Texas, which, in those days, was an even more racist city than its near neighbour, Dallas. 'Because,' says Granz, 'Houston was a much tougher city, and a much more prejudiced city ... it was a difficult city to break open.'

Norman Granz did what he always did: he rented the auditorium and took complete control. First he hired some of the local police (white, of course), to make quite sure there would be no trouble; then he removed the offensive signs which read 'White Toilets' and 'Negro Toilets', and then he told the ticket seller that tickets were to be sold on a first come, first served basis – there was to be no segregation whatsoever. Well, that was new for Houston all right. And to customers who found themselves in mixed company and wanted to change their seat, he'd say: 'No. Here's your money back. You sit where I sit you. If you say I don't like this seat because I can't hear, fine. But don't tell me there's a cat sitting next to you, and because he's black, you don't wanna sit there. You don't wanna sit there, here's your money back.' Granz knew the strength of his show, and he knew he could fill the house for two shows, many times over. 'People wanna see your show, you can lay some conditions down.'

Well, the show got started, and it all seemed to be going along nice and smoothly, when Granz noticed three young men lurking about backstage. Now it was a strict rule at JATP concerts that no visitors were allowed backstage during the show. Granz demanded to know who they were, and they produced badges which showed them to be plain-clothes policemen (the locals call them 'crackers'). They explained that they were not on duty, gosh, no! What they were was terrific jazz fans, and they were just there to cop a free look at the show. Outta sight, man! Granz grudgingly agreed to let them stay, provided that they stood well back and tried not to get in anybody's way.

Meanwhile, in Ella Fitzgerald's dressing room, a bunch of the boys were taking their ease between sets. There was Lester Young, Illinois Jacquet and Dizzy Gillespie, and they were doing what musicians always do when there's an hour to spare and nowhere to go – some play cards, some scrape reeds or oil valves – in this case, they were down on the floor, shooting dice. There was a nice little pot going too – about $185 – and Ella and her maid Georgianna were eating pie and drinking coffee and watching the game.

Suddenly, the door burst open, and in came the three jazz

loving crackers, waving guns and flashlights, and yelling, 'You're all under arrest for gambling.' The commotion brought Granz running, and the first thing he saw was one of the cops picking up the money from the floor, and another of them going into the bathroom. 'And I knew what it was then. I knew he was going to try and plant some shit. That's the first thing. That's for openers. Then it's easy, you see. "Black musicians caught ..." Good headlines.'

Granz followed the cop into the bathroom, and that got him rattled. 'What are you doing?' he demanded to know. 'I'm watching you,' said Granz. Whereupon, the cop completely lost his cool. He pushed his gun into Norman's stomach, and growled, 'I oughta kill you.' Everybody froze, and Ella and Georgianna began to cry. Granz said, 'Well, man, you've got the gun. If you want to shoot me, there's nothing I can do about it.' The moment passed, and one of the cops said, 'Okay, you're all under arrest, and we're taking you all to the station.'

By this time, the theatre manager had joined them. Granz turned to him. 'Right,' he said. 'I'm calling the show off, right now. You go out there and tell the people that the concert's finished, right now. And there'll be no second show because we've been arrested by the police. And you can settle the riot you're gonna have on your hands.' The manager began to tremble. He had visions of what might happen: a packed house of angry and frustrated fans, ripping up his seats – and there were another couple of thousand of them waiting patiently outside for the second show. He held a hasty conference with the forces of the law, and came back with the suggestion that Granz allow the show to finish. 'They'll take you down between concerts. 'Cause they're gonna have to book you. But they'll get you back in time for the second.'

Somehow or other, Lester Young missed the 'pinch', but Ella, Georgianna, Dizzy, Illinois and Norman Granz, all went down to the police station. Ella remembers it all too vividly: 'They took us down, and then when we got down there, they had the nerve to ask for an autograph! That was quite an experience.'

And Granz noticed a funny thing: the press were already there – reporters, photographers, everybody. It was all too obvious that the whole charade had been carefully arranged. It was a set-up. And the reasons were equally obvious: the Houston police perceived mixed audiences as a threat to the cherished status quo, which had to be resisted at all costs. 'All they wanted to do was create an incident,' says Granz. 'I mean they could have gotten us on drinking backstage, anything.'

Dizzy Gillespie, Illinois Jacquet, Ella and Georgianna were all charged with illegal gambling, and Granz, as the man responsible for them, with running an illicit gaming house! Ella was wearing her stage costume – as Dizzy remembers it, 'a pretty blue taffeta gown and a mink stole' – and she just kept crying and repeating that all she was doing was eating pie and watching the boys play their game. But they fingerprinted her with the others and locked them all in a cell. Dizzy was his usual cocky self. When they asked him his name, he said, 'Louis Armstrong.' And that's what they wrote down!

Bail was set at ten dollars, so Granz put up the fifty dollars for all of them. 'Well now,' says Granz, 'they knew we were leaving the next day; we're doing one-nighters. We were like in Detroit the next day. So it was a jive way of saying, "Now you've got a record down here for gambling. You don't show up you'll forfeit the bond, which means you'll be guilty and you'll lose the ten dollars."'

All this nonsense had taken but half an hour, and then they returned to the theatre to do the second show. But Granz hadn't finished with the Houston police, in fact, he had barely started. Says Dizzy, admiringly, 'He just wouldn't be intimidated by these people.' The following morning, Granz called a press conference, and gave the assembled newsmen a graphic, blow by blow account of what had happened. To their credit, one Houston paper wrote that the Houston police force should get a medal – it should be a chicken on a field of yellow.

The JATP left Houston to continue their tour, and Granz delivered the *coup de grâce*. He hired the best lawyer in Texas, fought the case, and won. It cost him over $2000 in legal fees, but the police were ordered to return the fifty dollar bond, and wipe the record clean. The lawyer proved that the police had had no right to enter the dressing room without a warrant. Well that's that, thought Granz. We'll never play Houston again. But they did. They went there the following year. And, says Granz, 'nobody touched us.'

In 1955, Norman Granz and his enterprises were grossing more than five million dollars a year. As John Hammond observed, he had done it by 'ignoring new trends and recording many of the best, and, ironically, least well known of the older jazz stars. As impresario he assembled casts of memorable players from the 1930s and 1940s ... putting on concerts in the finest halls and seeing to it that everyone who worked for him was well paid, well treated, and well appreciated.' There was, however, one sour note in the otherwise harmoniously rising cadence of Norman Granz's life – it was that Ella Fitzgerald's long standing arrangements with Decca prevented him from recording her, either in the studio or live at his concerts. Again and again he tried to buy back her contract, and each time, Decca refused.

So sure was he that Ella's Decca recordings were a disaster ('Santa Claus Got Stuck In My Chimney' indeed!), that he even began to suggest ideas for what she *might* record instead. Among those suggestions was a collection of songs by America's most distinguished composer of popular music, to be called *The Cole Porter Song Book*. Oh, no, no, no, no, no, said Milt Gabler – or words to that effect. That most definitely is not Ella Fitzgerald's kind of thing.

The most galling part was that Decca, along with all the other record companies, were no longer seriously interested in Ella Fitzgerald, or, come to that, in Bing Crosby, Frank Sinatra and the rest of the established favourites. They were too busy wooing a brand new audience – the post-war teenagers: millions of war babies, with ideas of their own and money in their pockets, who were about to make the million-selling record a commonplace. When RCA recorded Elvis Presley in 'Love Me Tender' in 1956, they booked 856,327 orders even before the record had reached the stores. The age of Rock was about to begin.

Then an opportunity arose which Norman Granz was too shrewd not to exploit. Universal Pictures, who had recently acquired the Decca Recording Company, decided to make a film about the life of Benny Goodman. Featured in the film as members of Goodman's band were Gene Krupa and a young tenor sax player named Stan Getz. They were both regular members of the JATP team, and they were both under exclusive contract to Granz.

Granz did nothing about that until Universal had completed their film, *The Benny Goodman Story*, and were about to launch the soundtrack album on Decca. Only then did he make his move. He told Universal that they couldn't release their album without his permission. When the inevitable haggle began, Granz stated his terms: he would grant his permission on one condition – that Decca terminate Ella Fitzgerald's recording contract forthwith. Decca were only too happy to agree.

Ella had not been lucky with the movies; since *Ride 'Em Cowboy*, a soggy comedy which had disappeared from sight as the popularity of its stars, Abbott and Costello, waned, she had done nothing on film of any consequence. It was not surprising really, since she was no Lena Horne or Peggy Lee; Ella's art was all for the ear, with little for the eye.

Late in 1955, however, a nice job turned up. Jack Webb had made a name for himself as director and star of what was to be a seminal tough city cop TV series called *Dragnet*. In '52 he had made a movie version of it, and now he was preparing to film a story about a jazz musician, called *Pete Kelly's Blues*. It was to be something of a labour of love, since Webb was a great jazz fan, and was quite knowledgeable on the subject.

Ella liked the idea enormously, but she became quite agitated when she learned that the film was to be shot in what was then a new and exciting process called Cinemascope. She had heard that the long letter-box shaped screen made those who appeared on it look enormous. Webb did his best to allay her fears. 'Just don't worry about it, honey,' he said. 'If it does it to you, it'll do it to me too.'

The musical director was Ray Heindorf, who had just finished recording the music for Judy Garland's *A Star Is Born*; and Sammy Cahn came in to write the lyric for the title song. When it was ready, they moved straight into the studio to record it, and Webb was mightily impressed with how Ella mastered the song, with practically no rehearsal, and sang it to perfection on the very first take.

It was Frank Sinatra in 1953, who had set the tone for the new era of long-playing records. Emerging from a long period in the shadows, he had recorded for Capitol in Hollywood three collections of songs with orchestral accompaniment, which had been an immediate hit and had gone a long way towards restoring his fortunes.

The elements which contributed to the success of those albums were several: firstly, there was Sinatra's own taste and judgement where popular music was concerned. He had found the current product of Tin Pan Alley vulgar and worthless, and so had looked backwards for his material to the great composers of Broadway musicals, from whose catalogues of songs he unearthed treasures long forgotten: 'My Funny Valentine' and 'Little Girl Blue' by Richard Rodgers; 'A Foggy Day' and 'Nice Work If You Can Get It' by George Gershwin; 'Just One Of Those Things' and 'At Long Last Love' by Cole Porter; 'I Won't Dance' by Jerome Kern.'

Secondly, his musical accompaniments were in the hands of an NBC staff arranger named Nelson Riddle, who put together a forty piece combination of top studio musicians (Hollywood's session men were the finest in the world), which combined the attributes of a swinging dance band and a classical string orchestra. Lastly, Sinatra had perceived that the fifteen or sixteen tracks needed some unifying theme to justify their inclusion on a long playing record; he and his Capitol advisors came up with *Songs For Young Lovers*, and *A Swinging Affair*.

The lessons to be learned from Sinatra's example were not lost on Norman Granz when the time came for Ella Fitzgerald to cut her first records under his management. Without hesitation he returned the idea which had been so dismissively rejected by Decca. He went into the studio with Ella to record what would be called *Ella Fitzgerald Sings The Cole Porter Song Book*.

First came the altogether daunting task of choosing, from among Porter's several hundred compositions, the songs which Ella would sing on the album. The richness of the material all but overwhelmed them, and eventually, having reduced the list as far as seemed possible, Granz decided to record not one album, but two – containing thirty-two titles. As musical director he chose Buddy Bregman, a young musician, brother to the songwriter Jule Styne, who was successfully conducting and arranging for NBC and CBS television shows in Hollywood.

When the tapes had been edited, Norman Granz took them to New York, in order to play them for the founder of the feast himself, Cole Porter. Porter lived in some considerable splendour in the Waldorf Towers, the exclusive residential wing of the Waldorf Astoria Hotel on Park Avenue. He had been an invalid since 1937, when a fall from a horse had crippled him, and since when he had been confined to a wheelchair, often, it was said, in much pain.

A butler greeted Granz's arrival – a humbling start to what might prove to be a nerve-wracking occasion. For it was well known that Cole Porter had little patience with singers and musicians who took vocal and instrumental liberties with his work. Especially the lyrics; the words were sacrosanct. There is a story that Porter was invited to visit the studio when Frank Sinatra was recording one of his songs: 'I Get A Kick Out Of You'.

> I get no kick from champagne,
> Mere alcohol
> Doesn't thrill me at all,
> So tell me, why should it be true?
> That I get a kick out of you.
> Some get a kick from cocaine,
> I'm sure that if
> I took even one sniff,
> It would bore me terrific'lly too;
> But I get a kick out of you.

Porter listened respectfully while the finest interpreter of popular songs of his generation sang the verse, followed by the first sixteen bars of the refrain. When Sinatra started the second sixteen with the words: 'Some they may go for cocaine . . .', the composer stirred uneasily in his wheelchair. And when, in an extended ending to the song, Sinatra sang: 'I get a kick – you give me a *boot* . . .', Porter had heard enough. He turned to his man and growled, 'Get me out of here.'

Cole Porter greeted Norman Granz with great courtesy. Together they listened to the tapes – all thirty-two tracks. Not a word was spoken. As Charles Fox observes in the sleeve note to the album: 'Ella certainly takes liberties with several of the songs – "It's All Right With Me" is a good example – adorning, embellishing, swinging the material as she was accustomed to do from the very outset of her career, yet the words remain inviolate.'

When the last track had been played, Porter turned to Norman Granz and said, 'What diction she has.'

Early in 1956, Norman Granz once again reorganized his recording business. Henceforth, everything would appear under a new label to be called Verve. It was destined to become the most important imprint in the history of American jazz recording. *Ella Fitzgerald Sings The Cole Porter Song Book* appeared on the new label, and sales immediately took off. Within months it had become the eleventh best selling album of the year.

In August 1956, Ella went into the studio to record with Louis Armstrong, accompanied by Oscar Peterson, Buddy Rich, Herb Ellis and Ray Brown. Their album, called *Ella and Louis* was another substantial hit, and it was quickly followed by a two-record, thirty-four track set, in which Ella explored the words and music of Richard Rodgers and Lorenz Hart. In June of the following year, she was back in the studio to record a four LP set called *Ella Fitzgerald Sings The Duke Ellington Song Book*.

Ella and Duke were old friends. They had appeared together at the Apollo in 1943, and she, like all the other women whose path had crossed his, had been the target of the sly, affectionate Ellington charm. Don George remembers a moment in the dressing room when, as Duke and Ella sit chatting, 'Lena Horne drops in unexpectedly to visit, wearing an attractive hat. Duke rises to the occasion. "You sure make that hat look pretty." Ella waves a disdainful hand. "Don't pay any attention to him, honey. He talks like that to everybody."'

On her *Duke Ellington Song Book*, Ella sings thirty-seven Ellington or Ellington associated songs. In eighteen of them she is accompanied by the big band, and in the rest by small groups. Whitney Balliet, in his *New Yorker* review, opines that 'the secret of jazz singing seems to be lost.' He continues: 'When Miss Fitzgerald got started as a jazz singer, in the mid-thirties, with Chick Webb, she had a thin, piping, highly rhythmic voice. Since then, it has gradually broadened into a deep contralto, and she has developed a technique that enables her to slide effortlessly up and down the scales, manage large intervals, and maintain perfect pitch. At the same time, her voice has taken on a soft edge that often blots out whatever jazz expression it once had. All the mannerisms of the jazz singer are there – an intensely

112

rhythmic delivery, plenty of embellishment, and unfailing drive and enthusiasm – but they are only an extremely skilful overlay that invariably leaves her materials unchanged. She is a peerless popular singer.'

In July and August, Ella was back again with Louis for *Ella and Louis Again*, and an album of the songs from Gershwin's *Porgy and Bess*, with the Russell Garcia orchestra. Both albums were successful, but Granz was far from satisfied. Later he complained to John McDonough of *Down Beat*, that he always seemed to get Louis at the worst possible times: 'We'd work for months to set everything up then – at the last moment we'd find he'd have a concert somewhere that evening. Everything would have to be rushed.' Also, Armstrong's lip, always in bad shape, was by that time making it almost impossible for him to play the trumpet. 'There was one session with orchestra backgrounds where it was so bad he practically had to sing the whole thing. I felt so sorry. He was playing almost entirely from one side of his mouth.'

The Ellington sessions were another disappointment to him. He told McDonough that the four LP album had been made under the most trying conditions. '[Duke] was under contract to Columbia, but I had Johnny Hodges [lately Ellington's celebrated lead alto player]. When Hodges rejoined the band in 1956 I managed to force a few concessions. I would have Duke for one LP or two if I used Ella. We planned far in advance, but in the end Duke failed to do a single arrangement. Ella had to use the band's regular arrangements. She'd do a vocal where an instrumental chorus would normally go. To stretch it to four LP's, we padded it with various small group things with Hodges, Ben Webster and so on.'

Ellington, however, must have enjoyed working with Ella, because not long after, he recorded an album of his own – a four movement work which he called *A Portrait of Ella Fitzgerald*, written in collaboration with his close associate since 1939, the gifted Billy Strayhorn. Duke speaks on the record, and in his introduction to the movement he calls

'Beyond Category', he intones, in his habitual orotund fashion: 'Ella Fitzgerald is a great philantropist. She gives so generously of her talent, not only to the public, but to the composers whose works she performs. Her artistry always brings to mind the words of the Maestro, Mr Toscanini, who said concerning singers, "Either you're a good musician or you're not." In terms of musicianship, Ella Fitzgerald is "Beyond Category".'

Duke Ellington was not alone in offering Ella such fulsome compliments. In 1957 and 1958, it seems that all the glittering prizes were hers. In both those years she won the *Metronome* poll, the *Playboy* poll, the *Down Beat* poll, and that magazine's Critics' Award. Norman Granz kept his promise to introduce her to the world of smart supper clubs and expensive restaurants. He booked her into the Copacabana in New York, an engagement without precedent for an artist of her race. And in 1958, Granz organized the 'Ella Fitzgerald Night at the Hollywood Bowl', when, with an orchestra of 108 musicians, she entertained an audience of 22,000 in that vast arena 'under the stars', and returned a year later to do it again. So exalted had Ella Fitzgerald become, so high her asking price, that from 1958 on, Norman Granz could no longer afford to present her as just another member of the Jazz At The Philharmonic troupe. She was a star, a main attraction, whose name on the marquee of a theatre was enough to draw a huge audience.

There were jazz festivals at Newport and Monterey, a Carnegie Hall concert with Duke Ellington to commemorate the release of her *Song Book* album, a guest appearance on NBC television, in Benny Goodman's *Swing Into Spring* show, and tours with the Oscar Peterson trio of Japan, Sweden, France and England.

Such a prodigious work-load might have floored a lesser person; Ella simply thrived on it. She was forty years old, she weighed more than two hundred pounds, and insisted that she didn't care who knew it. All the same, when a London reporter gallantly suggested that she looked slimmer than when last he'd seen her, she expressed enormous pleasure; 'Oh, thank you, thank you. That's the sweetest thing you've said today.'

True, the killing pace of JATP tours was greatly allevi- ated by the Norman Granz policy of first-class travel and the best available accommodation, and it is equally true that as queen of the entourage, Ella benefited most from the impresario's protective arm. Nevertheless it was hard going. Still, with air tickets booked and hotel suites ready and waiting, all blows were softened, all difficulties smoothed out.

Her off-duty pleasures were few and simple. Happiness, say touring musicians, is a town where you haven't seen the movie – Ella headed for the cinema every chance she got, and might stay there until show time. She sometimes sat through a favourite film three times. She also loved to sleep. Said Granz, 'She dotes on interior-sprung mattresses.'

Rarely moved to anger, Ella came closer to losing her temper on a morning when Jazz At The Philharmonic flew in to London Airport from France, on the first day of a fifteen-day concert tour of Britain. As Norman Granz, Oscar Peterson, Coleman Hawkins, Roy Eldridge, Ray Brown, Sonny Stitt, Stan Getz, Ella and the rest of the company made their way to the Customs Hall, they were not to know that Her Majesty's Customs Officers, frightened by lurid tales of the rackety life-styles of U.S. jazz men, were preparing to give their visitors the full treatment.

Having cleared the rest of the passengers, they got cracking on JATP's baggage. They searched everything, and that included instrument cases, saxophone bells, guitar 'f' holes – they even searched cigarette packets. They slit Norman Granz's toothpaste, and Ray Brown was made to strip, and had his vitamin pills impounded for analysis.

As for Ella, her entire wardrobe was meticulously exam- ined, and somebody had the bright idea of unstitching the lining of one of her coats. This humiliating process took an hour and a half to complete – longer than it had taken to fly from Paris.

What were they looking for? The Customs men wouldn't

115

say. But this was 1958, and the air was heavy with sinister portents. The country was still in shock over a film called *Rock Around The Clock*, in which Bill Haley and his Comets had so aroused its adolescent audience (they had yet to be yclept 'teenagers'), that they had leapt to their feet, uttered hoarse cries and danced in the aisles! Who knows what alien substances were coursing through their veins to provoke such manic behaviour? Oh, things were changing in '58. Chuck Berry was singing about 'Johnny B. Goode', Elvis was undulating his pelvis in 'Jailhouse Rock', and Jerry Lee Lewis was pounding his piano and screaming that there was 'a whole lotta shakin' goin' on.' (Had the customs men but known it, the worst was yet to come: John Lennon was still a Liverpool art student, and Mick Jagger, wearing winkle-picker shoes, was queueing up outside the Marquee Club in Wardour Street.)

Ella stormed out of the Customs Hall to a waiting car. 'I've been in a million places,' she growled. 'But I've never, never been put through anything like that.' And snapped at an importunate newsman: 'I wouldn't like to say at the moment that I'm glad to be here.'

7

In the early hours of Friday, July 17th, 1959, in a hospital in Harlem, Billie Holiday died. She was forty-four. The cause of her death was given as cirrhosis of the liver, complicated by a serious kidney infection. Nobody could say to what extent the addiction to drugs and alcohol which had tortured her for most of her adult life, had contributed to her death. She was buried on July 21st, and mourned by the whole of the jazz world. John Chilton, in *Billie's Blues* wrote: 'During her lifetime, Billie had cursed at, and quarrelled with, most of those who went in procession for the interment at St Raymond's Cemetery in the Bronx, but none bore her a grudge. Throughout most of her life, Billie had been her own worst enemy; the self-destructive demon within her had finally won.'

Her last years had been bitter and hard. Barred from working in New York clubs because of her conviction for drug offences, she had been rescued by Norman Granz who signed her to record for Verve, and arranged concert tours in Europe. She had quarrelled with him too, and Granz, uncharacteristically, was known to sound off angrily about Billie's maddening unpunctuality and her frequent skirmishes with the police, both of which he was inclined to interpret as just plain ingratitude.

It was inevitable that people would contrast Billie Holiday's hectic career and tragic end, with the calm, ordered and disciplined life of her near contemporary, Ella Fitzgerald. Rosetta Reitz, a record producer, told Kitty Grime that the differences between them were largely due to the steadying influences that Ella had always had: 'Chick Webb was very protective of Ella ... And Norman Granz later on was

117

very protective. Maybe, like so many singers, her love-life was kind of disappointing, but her work hasn't been ruined, like Billie's was.'

Ella's work, her reputation, her career were in fact, about to reach their highest peak. After more than a year of preparation, Norman Granz was about to release her finest album yet. It was entitled *Ella Fitzgerald Sings The George and Ira Gershwin Song Book*. The arrangements were written, and the orchestra conducted by Nelson Riddle, confirming the reputation already established with the Sinatra albums; and for the sleeve designs for the five record boxed set, Granz commissioned a School of Paris painter named Bernard Buffet, who was enjoying a tremendous vogue at the time. Norman Granz's huge success as a jazz impresario had given him the freedom to indulge his second most compelling enthusiasm, his love of modern art, and he had already begun to assemble a number of paintings by Picasso, which would eventually rival that of the biggest private collectors.

As a final touch, he produced, in the manner of the art world, a limited edition of Ella's latest songbook; only 175 copies, each of them bearing the autographs of Ira Gershwin, Nelson Riddle, Bernard Buffet and Ella herself.

In 1957, Norman Granz looked around at the American jazz scene and decided that he'd had enough of it. Jazz At The Philharmonic would no longer tour the United States. There were many reasons for his decision: during the past two years, first Charlie Parker and then Art Tatum had died, and Lester Young, the sweet and gentle Prez, was destroying himself with drink and marijuana. Buddy Rich, bored with the frenzied drum battles which were a feature of every JATP show, had denounced the whole circus to *Down Beat* as a 'load of junk', and Granz had replied angrily and in kind. True, Rich had rejoined the outfit, but then, what else could he do? JATP was practically the only game in town.

And the audiences were changing; the young were following new heroes now. What could a dedicated jazz buff like

Norman Granz make of a phenomenon like Elvis Presley? How do you react to something like 'You Ain't Nothin' But A Hound Dog'? Are they serious? Those twanging, clanking, three-chord, know-nothing, idiot-child guitar players; are they the ones who will replace the skills and the artistry of such as Barney Kessel and Herb Ellis? God help us all!

He liked what he saw and heard in the jazz world no better. Dizzy Gillespie was okay – beside being a brilliantly creative player, he was also an inspired clown with a warm hearted desire to please his audience – but the 'new Messiah' was Miles Davis, and Miles's cool was altogether too detached, too cerebral for Granz's tastes. As for Ornette Coleman, Free Jazz, and all that stuff, he told Leonard Feather: 'My reaction to his music is zero – whether it's some lack on my part or not, I really don't know.'

Other things had changed in the 50s too. Of that decade, John Hammond has written: 'Discrimination against Negroes virtually vanished from the music industry. Mixed jazz groups became the rule rather than the exception.' Both he and Granz could take much of the credit for that, but Granz battled on. His favourite restaurant in New York was the very grand and very expensive Le Pavillon, which maintained a rigid colour bar. Granz brought his two top clients, Oscar Peterson and Ella Fitzgerald, to lunch there, and Le Pavillon was forced to change its policy.

An event of September 1957 may have helped Norman Granz to decide to abandon the American tours. Louis Armstrong was in his hotel room in Grand Fork, North Dakota, during a tour with his All Stars, when he switched on the television set and caught what was happening in Little Rock, Arkansas in the course of the schools desegregation programme. In horror, he watched black pupils attempting to assert their rights in accordance with the Supreme Court ruling. Max Jones and John Chilton describe the incident in their book on Louis: '. . . One child was shown walking timidly up to the school building. As Louis watched her passing the line of jeering whites, a man moved forward and spat in the girl's face. It was a moment of shock

119

for the viewer, too, like a blow in the face. He got mad and stayed mad.'

Louis gave a newspaper interview denouncing President Eisenhhower ('no guts'), the Governor of Arkansas, Orval Faubus ('an uneducated ploughboy'), and the whole United States government ('the Government can go to hell'). Coming from a famous man with no record of militancy, Armstrong's attack found its mark. Eisenhower was forced to act immediately, and the story goes that he never, ever forgave Louis.

All this sparked off a lively debate in the entertainment world about whether Louis' outburst had been justified or not. Both Leonard Feather and Dave Brubeck cancelled Southern dates where managements banned desegregated seating. Norman Granz, who had never booked such dates for Jazz At The Philharmnonic, added his voice in Louis' defence.

Whatever the reasons, Granz had become disenchanted with his native land, and in 1959 he upped sticks and moved to Geneva, returning only occasionally to look after Oscar and Ella and their flourishing careers.

Two things happened that year which may have had something to do with Granz's decision to leave. Elvis Presley returned from his two-year haul with the U.S. Army and made two records; one, 'It's Now Or Never' sold nine million copies, the other, 'Are You Lonesome Tonight', sold a mere five million. His first TV appearance, a guest shot on a Frank Sinatra special, commanded a hitherto unheard of fee of $125,000. The other thing that happened was the great payola scandal. A Congressional Investigative Committee established that disc jockeys, the new lords of the air, were receiving payment for plugging records. One of them, Dick Clark, was revealed as having interests in no less than thirty-three record and publishing firms, which provided him with an income of half a million dollars! Granz, of course, was not involved – nobody was going to pay good money for plugging a jazz record, for God's sake – all the same, the event marks the beginning of his disenchantment with the recording business, and he started to think seriously about selling Verve.

Meanwhile, Ella had moved into a new home in Los Angeles, a modest enough seven-room two-storeyed house (with the obligatory Beverly Hills swimming pool), of which she was immensely proud. She had helped decorate it, and there was a garden in which she loved to potter. There was a gleamingly new kitchen – always a joy for those who spend much of their lives in faraway places with strange sounding (and tasting) menus – but especially for Ella, whose fondness for food was legendary. Fried chicken, honeyed hams and watermelon, the staples of traditional Southern cooking, were her favourites, but for Ella, chow time was simply any time, any place. Sammy Cahn, the songwriter, remembers her at a Decca recording session in 1938: 'She was standing at the microphone with a hot dog in one hand, and a bottle of coke in the other. It was a ballad she was about to record, a song that required some kind of feeling, some personal involvement. She couldn't wait to get at the song so she could eat.'

On those rare days when she could enjoy the luxury of relaxing in her very own home, her favourite pastimes were 'lots of good listening to good records, shopping for the house, going to movies, and nice, relaxed, at home gab sessions with my friends.' There was also her son, Ray Junior, now ten years old, with whom she liked to spend as much time as possible. She helped him with his homework and fussed over his needs. Somewhat wistfully she confesses, 'I'm a home-body.'

A 'home-body' was how she may have seen herself, but that was just what there simply wasn't time to be. The demands of her career were carrying her further away from home, and for longer periods of time, than ever before. JAPT may have abandoned America, but Europe, Latin America and the Far East still welcomed Norman Granz's jamming musicians, and now Ella had become the undisputed star of the show. In fact, her progress around the concert halls of London, Paris, Stockholm, Copenhagen, Berlin, Buenos

121

Aires and Tokyo, now resembled a royal tour, her reception ecstatic, her command absolute.

When she opened a British tour at London's Royal Festival Hall, the late Kenneth Allsop was moved to eulogize her thus: 'Bulky and almost gauche in manner, and spending a good deal of time and breath on pops and ballads not strictly within the jazz sphere, she yet transports the material and the occasion to the level of greatness. Her voice lilts like a lark's and swells with organ sadness, is tender and then wry with the finest swerve, and she has a bat-like sensitivity of ear which enables her to skim dazzlingly above the surface of a song with never a momentary muff.'

Two years later, in 1961, announcing the beginning of another British tour, Robin Douglas-Home wrote in the *Daily Express*: 'Tomorrow, with no attempt at showmanship or stagecraft, she will be holding her audiences spellbound by just standing – and singing. Eyes closed, thumb and forefinger of one hand clicking out the beat, the other hand clutching a wisp of orange silk to mop the sweat-beads on her brow ... Looking at her one might expect a deep, sonorous voice. But the sound is pure, almost child-like. The voice, now velvet, now husky, swoops and plunges with uncannily perfect control, caressing a phrase here, jumping an octave there. The texture is as airy and light as a willow-warbler's spring-song.'

That year, she returned to Europe for the third time in two years, playing, in London alone, fourteen concerts in seven days. They called her Ella, Queen of Song, the Maria Callas of the Blues, and, with reckless disregard for jazz distinctions, the Joan Sutherland of Dixieland. Allsop remarked that since Margot Fonteyn deserved to be a Dame Commander of the British Empire (an honour she had recently received), then Ella Fitzgerald should forthwith be appointed a Dame Commander of the World of Jazz.

Publicists and pressmen alike were fond of quoting Bing Crosby's alleged pronunciamento: 'Man, woman or child, Ella is the greatest.'

The success of Ella's *Cole Porter Song Book*, and of her duets with Louis Armstrong, had prompted Norman Granz to widen the scope of his Verve recordings to include material beyond his chosen field of classic jazz. To this end he had brought in other producers to handle the more commercial stuff. Buddy Bregman, who had arranged the music and conducted the orchestra for some of Ella's song books, recorded film stars like Jane Powell and Mitzi Gaynor. Barney Kessel, the guitarist, tried his hand at producing albums with Ricky Nelson, a bobby-soxer rave of the time, and they too became big sellers.

Added to this were the spoken word albums that Verve released with people like Evelyn Waugh and Dorothy Parker, and hugely successful comedy albums with Mort Sahl, Lennie Bruce and Jonathan Winters. By 1959, Verve was producing some 150 albums a year.

But it was characteristic of a man given to volatile enthusiasms, that the more successful Verve became, the less interested he became in running it, and in 1959, Norman Granz decided that the time had come to sell.

Frank Sinatra was about to leave Capitol, the company which had produced his biggest selling albums, and was in the market for a new recording company. However, among the conditions of his purchase of Verve was his insistence that Granz remain as a full time executive, and since Granz had already moved to Switzerland, the offer did not appeal.

A better offer came soon enough. In 1960, Norman Granz sold Verve records to MGM for $2,800,000. The new owners hired a man named Creed Taylor to be the new executive director. Taylor immediately began remaking Verve in the MGM image – in other words, it was going to be strictly commercial. When you've spent that kind of money for something, it had better start earning its keep. Granz had agreed, for one year, to act as advisor on artists and repertoire, but when Taylor began by firing all Granz's contract artists, with the exception of Stan Getz, Johnny

123

Hodges, Oscar Peterson and Ella Fitzgerald, it soon became apparent that he could have little influence over the direction the new régime was taking.

Granz watched Verve's transformation with gloomy resignation. He told John McDonough of *Down Beat*: 'For better or worse the company stood for something when I left. But the new owners were lawyers and marketing people. I can't blame them for not caring as much as I did. It wasn't their work. And it would have been foolish of me to expect the company to have continued as before.' He fumed through most of the 60s, as he saw his artists discarded in favour of the new rock stars – groups like the Velvet Underground and the Mothers of Invention. He told Leonard Feather: 'It's criminal that someone like Sarah Vaughan was allowed to go without making a single record for five years. It's an outrage that of the twenty-seven albums I produced with Art Tatum for Verve, not a single one is available – they've all been deleted from the catalogue. The son of a bitch who did that ought to be hung from the nearest lamppost.'

It was not surprising that the jazz virtuosi should be brushed aside at such a time. In 1963, the first records by the Beatles had arrived in America, and the following year, the four Liverpool lads with their funny haircuts and their cocky charm had arrived in person to appear on the Ed Sullivan TV show. They played for a studio audience of 700, and a viewing audience of some 73,000,000. Their spot on the show lasted for five minutes, during which the fans in the studio screamed so loud that not a single note of what they played or sung was heard. When it was over, the dead-pan Ed Sullivan turned to camera, and said, 'America, judge for yourself.'

The one Verve artist seemingly unaffected by the new emphasis was Ella Fitzgerald. She continued to record regularly; four albums in 1960 – one, live from the Deutschland-Halle in Berlin, with the quartet she was touring with: Paul Smith on piano, Jim Hall on guitar, Wilfred Middlebrooks on bass and Gus Johnson on drums;

another, an album of Christmas songs with Frank de Vol's orchestra, and a third with only Paul Smith at the piano. And lastly, with Billy May's orchestra, another song book devoted to the music of Harold Arlen. Between 1961 and 1964, there were albums with the orchestras of Nelson Riddle and Marty Paitch; recordings made at the Crescendo Club in Los Angeles, in New York, in London, and at the Jazz Festival in Juan-Les-Pins. And again with Nelson Riddle, the *Jerome Kern Song Book*.

When not in the recording studio, she continued her stately progress around the world, although she had at last been persuaded to take life a little easier than heretofore. She now worked no more than thirty-five to forty weeks a year, pausing to refresh herself in Los Angeles, and in a small flat she had acquired in Klampenborg, a seaside resort just outside Copenhagen. She insisted on the convenient location of this pied-à-terre, because 'we always seem to be stopping here.' There was another reason which she confided to Leonard Feather: 'Because I had a romance there.' She kept the Klampenborg flat for four years.

Rationalize it how she might, the deadly treadmill of years of air travel, hotel living and performing were beginning, slowly but surely, to take their toll. She worried about her sinuses, which the constant changes of climate (especially the miserable dampness of northern English cities) aggravated mercilessly. She worried about her performance, agonizing over every note, every flaw, real or imagined, she thought may have marred it. 'Did you hear my voice getting hoarse in that number?' she asked Max Jones. 'I was going up, and had to change my mind.'

In March 1965, in Munich, in the middle of her act, she suddenly lost control. She faltered, stopped singing and had to be led from the stage. The audience, sensing something wrong, sat silent for a while, then began to applaud. Nobody left the hall. When Ella had regained her composure, she returned to the stage and finished the set.

From Germany, she continued on to England, where, reluctantly, on her doctor's insistence, she cancelled some of her London concerts. But the real therapy was work. 'I feel different the moment I get on the stage,' she told Margaret Laing of the *Sunday Times*. Even so, she was beginning to be persuaded that, as her doctor had warned, she must be prepared to say NO. 'We go at such a pace,' she said wearily. 'You run to eat dinner because in some hotels the restaurant closes at 11.30 p.m. I don't like to eat between shows, it makes me short-winded.' She described a typical schedule: 'On the Continent we were sometimes at the second concert until 3 a.m. – in Frankfurt it was 4.30 – and then had to get up early to catch a plane. In Amsterdam, we did a midnight show, then flew to Warsaw to appear that night. A concert artist would never agree to do as we do. I don't think it's fair. People are still paying – so you should be able to do the show right.' Some weeks had passed since her unseemly lapse in Munich, but she was still brooding over it. 'Some people get very angry when you're ill,' she said. 'But working every day on a voice, you can't expect it to be perfect. It's a God-given talent – you shouldn't abuse it. I don't think I want to any more.' Ella was learning to say no. She returned to her haven in Los Angeles, and for most of the rest of 1965, she settled down to the serious business of recharging her batteries.

In 1965, Ella Fitzgerald had no hit record, and it wasn't hard to see why. 'The times,' Bob Dylan was singing, 'they are a-changin',' and he was right. Mick Jagger of the Rolling Stones was petulantly screaming, 'I can't get no satisfaction.' And the Who were talking about 'my generation'. Between them, these young men were selling records, and every album the Beatles recorded was 'going gold' the moment it hit the stores. Promoters had given up concert halls and were hiring football stadiums, race tracks and ball parks in which to accommodate the vast crowds who would assemble to worship their new idols.

Norman Granz complained about the way record companies had changed. 'Executives nowadays are only concerned with the fact that they can gross nine million dollars with the Rolling Stones. They forget that a profit is still a profit, that you still make money if you only net nine thousand.'

Ella herself observed the changing scene and found much of it baffling. Particularly, she was worried by what seemed to her the too easy attainments of the new stars. To Leonard Feather she said: 'When I started with Chick I made 25 dollars a week. Two years later it was 75 dollars, and when I finally got to 125 dollars it was a big thrill. Nowadays they make a record that hits overnight and boom, they're million-aires before they've even had a chance to study music.' When the conversation touched on the Beatles and their phenomenal success, she refused to put them down: 'I don't care what people say about the Beatles. They've proved they do know some kind of music and I'd love to make an album of their songs.' Her son, Ray Junior, now attending Beverly Hills High School, was playing weekend gigs as the drummer with what Ella described as a 'Ringo beat' combo – so she was well aware of how the popular music world was changing. There's nothing like having a teenager in the house to keep you in touch with the passing parade outside. Some years later, in London, she recorded a 'songbook' album of Lennon and McCartney songs, and as she always did, made them her own.

Norman Granz returned from Switzerland in 1967, for one last JATP tour of America. For the purpose he assem-bled a group which included all of his very special favourites. There was Benny Carter, now a venerable sixty years of age, and Coleman Hawkins, even older at sixty-three. Hawkins, that great musician, virtually the creator of modern tenor saxophone playing, had not much longer to live. He died in New York on May 19th, 1969. And of course, there were Granz's brightest stars, Oscar Peterson and Ella Fitzgerald. When the tour was over, Granz said, 'Never again. I made a profit, but it's too much of a production, too much work, and above all, too much aggravation. It's no fun any more, at least not in the States.'

Ella's eyes had been troubling her for some time. Bright lights made her blink, and she was especially bothered by the flash bulbs of news photographers. In 1971, she was found to have a cataract on her right eye, and an operation was ordered. It was completely successful, and Ella was delighted to find that she could now see her audiences better. 'I can reach them now and see how happy they feel.' She got herself some contact lenses, but they hurt her eyes when she was tired, so she switched to owl-like horn-rimmed spectacles, which she wore even when she worked.

But her troubles were not over. The following summer, while she was appearing in Verona, her left eye began to haemorrhage. She left immediately to consult with Dr Miller Berliner, an eminent eye specialist who summered each year in Monte Carlo. Dr Berliner's verdict was swift and conclusive: 'Unless she takes a very long rest, she is liable to lose her sight completely.' Norman Granz lost no time in cancelling all her engagements until the end of the year, and that included an autumn tour of Britain. So once again, an event beyond her control had forced her to take a long and much needed break.

When at last her doctor gave her permission to resume work, her happiness was boundless. 'When that doctor said okay,' she told Max Jones, 'I just grinned and went ahead. We rehearsed at home with the fellows and then performed in public. It seemed to me my voice had changed and was pitched way up somewhere, it was a strange feeling. But the fellows laughed and said the voice was all right.'

There had been another event, sombre and saddening, during her long lay off; it was the death on July 6th, 1971, of Louis Armstrong. Louis, with whom she had recorded some marvellous albums: *Ella and Louis, Ella and Louis Again* and *Porgy And Bess*. Louis, the Great Satchelmouth, the very spirit of jazz incarnate, was gone. *Down Beat*'s headline read: 'One of the great men of the 20th century is dead.' They printed a statement from the President; 'Mrs Nixon and I

128

share the sorrow of millions of Americans at the death of Louis Armstrong. One of the architects of an American art form, a free and individual spirit, and an artist of world wide fame, his great talents and magnificent spirit added riches and pleasure to all our lives.'

At the funeral on July 9th, Ella was one of the honorary pall bearers. The others included Bing Crosby, Pearl Bailey, Johnny Carson and Dizzy Gillespie. There was a simple service, and at Lucille Armstrong's request, the only music was Peggy Lee singing the Lord's Prayer. It was a solemn and dignified occasion. It was said that Louis would have liked a New Orleans jazz band, but his birthplace was a town whose rigid segregation laws had forced him to declare that he would never return there. In 1959 it was still impossible to present a band with mixed black and white personnel, and that effectively barred Louis' All Stars. 'I'm accepted all over the world,' he had said. 'And when New Orleans accepts me, I'll go home.' He did go home, at least in spirit, when the town honoured him with a memorial service. The bands played, and 15,000 people came to pay their respects.

Norman Granz, exasperated beyond endurance by what he regarded as the misuse of his favourite artists, decided to get back into the record business. First, he tried to buy back Verve, but MGM weren't interested. Then, in 1972, he promoted a concert in Santa Monica, with Ella Fitzgerald and Count Basie. He had been out of recording since the Verve sale. 'I don't know what possessed me to do it,' he says. 'But I decided to record it. While I was at it I decided to add a few surprise guests. Oscar was in town, and I brought in Stan Getz, Roy Eldridge, Harry Edison, Ray Brown and some others. It was a lot of fun and went well, so afterwards I thought I'd see how it might go as a record. I put out a small mail order thing and it was a disaster. Sold about a hundred and fifty. But a few got over to Europe and I got a call from Polydor saying they would give me world-wide distribution if I went back in the record business. It was too good to refuse.'

He set about creating a brand new record label which he called Pablo – a tribute to Pablo Picasso, whose works he had been acquiring at a furious rate whenever they came up for auction. In April, 1968, at Sotheby's in London, he put up for auction a large chunk of his collection: an assortment of modern painters and twenty-five of his Picassos. He told Derek Jewell, 'At first I bought madly, but now I know which two or three pictures contain the essence of the man for me. These I am keeping. I've balanced my portfolio.' The sale yielded £862,500.

There can be no doubt that Norman Granz had missed the fun and excitement of record producing. And now that he was back where the action was, he would use Pablo to translate his ideas into palpable achievement. He told Leonard Feather: 'It's a disgrace what jazz artists today are being forced to do, recording material that is all wrong for them. I let them try it with Ella and they wanted to create a new image for her by having her work the Fillmore [a rock venue in San Francisco] to promote this album of pop songs she'd recorded. I said "What for? She's making half a million a year as she is, why should I change that?" If I had my way Ella would never make another record – at least not by those standards. Who gives a damn?'

But he did give a damn, and Pablo soon became a jazz label without equal. He bought back from MGM all the Art Tatum sessions he had recorded. Sarah Vaughan, shamefully neglected for so long, recorded at least eight albums for Pablo, and restored herself to fame and fortune in the process. Others, too, came to record – Dizzy Gillespie, Joe Turner, the blues singer, and Benny Carter, sixty-five years old and still going strong.

Ella, once again, was given pride of place in the Pablo catalogue. Granz concentrated on his own particular contribution to jazz literature, the album recorded 'live' at concerts and jazz festivals. In 1972, there was *Jazz at the Santa Monica Civic*; in 1973 and 1975, albums from the Jazz

Festival at Montreux, a town on Lake Geneva. And again in 1977 – *Pablo, Live. Montreux,* with her favourite pianist, Tommy Flanagan, and his trio. There was *Ella in London, Ella in Berlin, Ella and Duke at the Côte d'Azur, Ella Fitzgerald/ Newport Jazz Festival, Live at Carnegie Hall* and *A Perfect Match,* Basie and Ella at Montreux in 1979.

There were studio albums with Joe Pass, a remarkably accomplished guitarist, with whom she often toured, an album with Oscar Peterson, and a rip-roaring jazz session with Tommy Flanagan, Joe Pass, Ray Brown, Louie Bellson, Zoot Sims, Eddie Davis, Clark Terry and Harry Edison.

There was another song book, this one devoted to the works of Antonio Carlos Jobim, the Brazilian composer of 'Quiet Nights of Quiet Stars' and 'The Girl from Ipanema', and in 1982, she was back in the studio with Nelson Riddle for *The Best Is Yet To Come.* For this album, Nelson Riddle created a wonderfully fresh orchestral sound. He explains: 'Norman said he was tired of the conventional sound of a violin section, so we agreed on the use of four flutes, eight celli and four French horns. By superimposing the flute or celli on the horns I was able to create a sound similar to the blend Debussy achieved in *La Mer.*'

The Best Is Yet To Come won for Ella her twelfth 'Grammy', the annual accolade awarded by the recording industry of America. Since 1972, Ella Fitzgerald has recorded twenty-three albums for Pablo, an astonishing achievement.

The scene is London; the time, June, 1985. André Previn, the American conductor, long resident in England, is about to assume the Music Directorship of the Royal Philharmonic Orchestra, and in celebration of the event, the orchestra will present a music festival at the Royal Festival Hall on London's South Bank. Joining the orchestra in the music of Mozart, Ravel, Mendelssohn, Beethoven and Brahms, will be Previn's favourite soloists, the pianists Vladimir Ashkenazy and Krystian Zimerman, the violinists Pinchas Zukerman and Kyung-Wha Chung, and the singers Lucia Popp and Thomas Allen. And representing the world of jazz will be Buddy Rich, Oscar Peterson and Ella Fitzgerald.

André Previn's alliance with such jazz virtuosi is no mere conceit; he has every right to number them among his friends. Born in 1929, in Berlin, he arrived with his family in America at the age of ten. By the time he had left High School he was a wunderkind pianist, and was working at the Metro Goldwyn Mayer studios in Hollywood, writing the orchestral scores for such films as *Gigi*, *Porgy and Bess*, and *Bells Are Ringing*. Between 1949 and 1955 he was recording for Victor, and his jazz version of the music from *My Fair Lady* in 1957 was a best seller. It is often said that for a musician to make the giant leap from jazz to classical music is an impossibility. If that is so, then Previn has achieved the impossible. Since 1960, his conducting career has encompassed every major orchestra in the world. He has been Musical Director of the Houston Symphony in succession to Sir John Barbirolli; was principal conductor for eleven years of the London Symphony Orchestra, and Music Director of

the Pittsburgh Symphony. He has appeared regularly with the Berlin Philharmonic, the Vienna Philharmonic and the symphony orchestras of Chicago, Boston and Philadelphia.

His first recordings with Ella Fitzgerald were for Decca in 1955, when he wrote a few arrangements and conducted a small string orchestra to back her in the songs 'You'll Never Know', 'Thanks For The Memory', 'It Might As Well Be Spring' and 'I Can't Get Started'. And then, in 1984, after an interval of almost thirty years, he was the sole accompaniment on a Pablo album called *Nice Work If You Can Get It*, on which Ella once again explores the words and music of George and Ira Gershwin.

Asked to comment on this unique experience, Previn said: 'The obvious and shocking fact about the intervening years is of course, that the passage of time has changed all of us with the exception of Ella. It may have deepened her voice a bit, but everything that was evident in 1955 is just as admirable in 1984. And I doubt very much if any of her millions of fans who decided she was the world's greatest jazz singer when they heard her with Chick Webb have found any reason to change their minds since. She is unique and inimitable, simply the best, and transcends any and all of the so-called barriers that supposedly exist between the various and disparate kinds of music.'

Ella flies into London from Paris on Wednesday, June 26th. She is tired and is suffering from a bad cold, the legacy of the worst June weather, wet and miserably cold, to have afflicted Europe for twenty years. Her contribution to the two-week André Previn Music Festival at the Festival Hall, will be a concert billed as 'Ella Fitzgerald and Friends', and it will be her last engagement in a long and exhausting European tour. She retires to her suite in the Grosvenor House Hotel in Park Lane, to recoup her forces and be ready for Friday evening.

The concert has been a complete sell out for weeks. All

133

three thousand Festival Hall seats have been bought and paid for, and on the night, five hundred hopeful fans will queue in front of the box office in the hope of snapping up returns. Ticket touts will lurk around the forecourt, offering seats which cost from five to fifteen pounds, at prices as high as a hundred pounds each.

By 7.15, the audience has assembled in the hall. They are for the most part young, brightly but decently dressed (the weather has at last turned June-like); pretty girls with their escorts, young men with well-trimmed hair who have come straight from some city office and will slide their briefcases beneath their seats. There is a pleasant murmur of conversation, modestly low-keyed, nothing shrill. This is a middle-class English audience, slightly over-awed by the grand dimensions of the Royal Festival Hall, and by the sense of special occasion.

The house lights go down, and attendants close the doors. As in the manner of classical music concerts which habitually take place here, latecomers will not be allowed to enter until applause at the end of a number signals the doormen to admit them.

Ella's accompanying trio, her friends of the bill matter, enter. They are led on to the platform by pianist Paul Smith, a sixtyish Californian – tall, dignified, with the look of a helpful bank manager. He is followed by Keter Betts, the bass player, and Bobby Durham, the drummer, Fitzgerald side-men since the early '70s. Ella, unannounced, follows immediately. The audience greet her warmly. They know her well, and the occasion is already sweetly familiar. Ella accepts the hand mike from Paul Smith, and she is into her opening number – 'Take The "A" Train'.

She is slimmer, with that slightly drawn look common to people who have determinedly lost weight. Having chosen her spot on the platform, she will remain there for most of the evening, her only bodily expression an occasional toss of the head, and her left hand slapping her hip to emphasize an off beat. The trio carry her along, accenting, embellishing; it is a lively conversation among close friends.

134

She segues into the Gershwins' 'They Can't Take That Away From Me.'

> The way you wear your hat,
> The way you si-hi-hi-hi-hip your tea...

The low and middle registers are warm and rich; only the high notes carry an undulous vibrato that she wishes she were better able to control. The audience relaxes, reassured; the famous voice is intact.

After her two opening numbers she pauses to greet the full house: 'We'll sing some old ones, and some new ones ... and some we don't know ...' She sings another ballad, 'Crazy in Love', and then she is into 'Lullaby of Birdland'. The audience recognizes the opening bars and applauds gratefully, anticipating a treat. Ella obliges in the second chorus with spirited scat singing. Is it quite as nimble, quite as neatly inventive as before? Is it perhaps a little raucous, a shade desperate? No matter. It is Ella, doing her old, familiar thing.

She does a medley of songs from *My Fair Lady*; she introduces her trio, Paul Smith, Keter Betts and Bobby Durham, who take modest bows. She sings 'Black Coffee', and is back in the land of scat. Playfully she interpolates a phrase from an old song: 'A-Tisket, A-Tasket, I lost my yellow basket ...' The audience applaud hopefully, but Ella nips the unspoken request in the bud, with a mock-stern admonition: 'And that's all you're gonna git!'

After the interval, the audience is surprised and delighted by the unannounced appearance on the platform of Joe Pass, the virtuoso guitarist. Pass is playing at Ronnie Scott's Club in Soho, and Norman Granz has persuaded him to join them at the Festival Hall. He plays 'I Can't Get Started' and 'Summertime'. After which, Ella joins him, and together they run through 'I'm Beginning To See The Light', 'A Foggy Day', 'Satin Doll' and 'One Note Samba'. They know each other so well, these two, admire each other's work so much, that they are able to challenge each other to playful feats of musical daring.

The trio returns to the platform, and Ella concludes her concert with 'Every Time We Say Goodbye'. The house lights go up, and attendants enter with bouquets of flowers. The applause is solid and prolonged, and brings Ella back for encores, a ritual oft repeated. 'Leave the lights up,' she commands. 'I want to see you all.' She sings 'Mack The Knife' and 'Miss Otis Regrets'. This time, as she leaves, the audience rises and there are a few cheers. Ella throws kisses, the audience begins to leave. They are content. The evening has been well spent. It has been a cosy, comfortable occasion – a couple of hours in the company of a favourite aunt. When next she comes to visit, they will be there to greet her.

Ella Fitzgerald has been a professional singer for half a century. For all but three of that great span of years, she has been a celebrity; as famous in Buenos Aires and Rio de Janeiro as she is in Tokyo, Hong Kong, Stockholm, Copenhagen, Berlin, Paris and London. She travels hundreds of thousands of miles every year, and has appeared in more countries than any artist of her own or any other time.

On gramophone records she has sung more than two thousand different songs, and, since the advent of the long playing record in the 1950s, she has made some seventy albums.

She works for forty weeks of every year, resting quietly for the remainder at her house in Beverly Hills, the same house she bought back in 1967. There are now two dogs, a housekeeper named Doreen, and cookbooks, stacks of them in almost every room. She told Leonard Feather, 'I've got them from all over the world. It's fascinating – like reading love stories – you find yourself comparing what different cooks will do with the same meats.'

At the age of sixty-seven, she gives no sign, either by word or deed, that she contemplates even a modification of her rigorous work schedule. Ella Fitzgerald will go on singing, because singing is her life.

Since her divorce from Ray Brown in 1953, she has not

remarried; although there have been stories about men in her life over the years. In 1957, it was a Norwegian artists' agent named Thor Larsen, ten years her junior, with whom her name was briefly linked. It was even rumoured that they had been married in Paris two years earlier. Thorsen denied it, and Joe Glaser in New York, answering reporters' queries, snapped, 'It's a lie. Not a word of truth in it.'

There is an element of wish-fulfilment about this. 'I get lonesome when I'm travelling,' she would say. That was in the old Jazz At The Philharmonic days, and Ray Brown was a member of the Oscar Peterson trio. She would look across at him, and say, wistfully. 'That's life. Mr Brown is a happily married man now.' Her son, Ray Brown Junior, is himself a married man now. He lives in Seattle, plays guitar and drums, and leads a band with a country music flavour. Ella has been told that he sings, but she has never heard him.

Nat Hentoff wrote, in *The Jazz Word*, 'Ella is a gentle, ingenuous woman. She is still startled that movie stars are among her fans.' When, in 1963, she was introduced to Elizabeth Taylor and Richard Burton in a London hotel, she was as thrilled as any teenage moviegoer. 'Wasn't that something? Isn't she just too beautiful? She was lovely to me. Brother, that's all that matters in life.' Her one regret was, spotting Liz's mink coat draped across the back of her chair, that she hadn't worn her own expensive furs for the occasion.

And Leonard Feather wrote: 'Totally in awe of her peers, she has a sense of everyone's importance but her own. Recalling with pride Tony Bennett's annual Christmas visits to her home, plus her own presence at Peggy Lee's New Year's Eve parties, she seems unaware that other singers (along with architects, brain surgeons and heads of state) are themselves reverential toward the First Lady of Song.'

A gentle and ingenuous woman. And, Hentoff adds, 'still trusting beyond most others' capacities to imagine trust.' Frank Sinatra sends her yellow roses when she appears with him on T.V. He is gentle and loving with her and she adores him. 'Warmth is the main thing in this life,' she says. 'Giving and getting warmth.' She expresses it through her work for under-privileged children; a child care centre in the Lynwood section of Los Angeles bears her name.

Her profession has honoured her with every award it has ever instituted. She has been voted best singer by the musical journals *Down Beat*, *Metronome* and *Melody Maker*, and by *Esquire* and *Playboy* magazines. The recording industry has awarded her its 'Grammy' on twelve occasions, many of them for her song book albums on Verve and Pablo. The most recent, for *The Best Is Yet To Come*, was presented to her at the twenty-sixth annual ceremony in the Shrine Auditorium in Los Angeles on February 28th, 1984.

The Kennedy Centre for the Performing Arts in Washington has presented her their Honors Medal. The Beverly Hills Chamber of Commerce has presented her with the Will Rogers Memorial Award, and she has been proclaimed Beverly Hills Woman of the Year. The American Society of Composers, Authors and Publishers (ASCAP) has presented her with its highest honour, the Pied Piper Award, and Lord and Taylor, the New York department store has presented her with its Rose Award. In 1982, Harvard's Hasty Pudding Club chose Ella as their Woman of the Year, greeting her with a standing ovation and a rousing chorus of 'A-Tisket, A-Tasket', and in 1984 she was the winner of the Whitney Young Award, sponsored by the National Association for the Advancement of Coloured People.

There are more honours: the dedication at the University of Maryland of the Ella Fitzgerald Auditorium of Performing Arts, an Honorary Doctorate of Humane Letters from Dartmouth College, a Doctorate of Music from Howard University, and a Doctorate of Humane Letters from Talledega College in Alabama.

On April 7th, 1983, the forty state senators, assembled for a regular session of the California Legislature, adopted Senate Resolution No. 19, which went, in part, as follows: WHEREAS, Jazz is a uniquely American musical institution that has produced some of the world's greatest musical talents and one of these musical giants is Ella Fitzgerald, whom many consider the Queen of Song; and WHEREAS, For nearly fifty years, Ella's inimitable style, graciousness, musical inventiveness, and unending musical genius have entertained audiences around the world; and WHEREAS, Ella Fitzgerald, the consummate musician, has made major contributions to the American musical scene, and Ella Fitzgerald, the person, has enhanced the quality of life of all having the pleasure of associating with her; now, therefore be it RESOLVED BY THE SENATE OF THE STATE OF CALIFORNIA, That the Members take great pleasure in honouring Ella Fitzgerald for her illustrious career and convey sincere best wishes for continued success and happiness in her future endeavours.

At home, then, she is a national treasure; and beyond the borders of her own country? 'She is one of the élite,' wrote Leonard Feather in the Los Angeles *Times*, 'for whom a single name on a marquee would suffice almost anywhere in the world.'

And how does a singer of popular songs achieve a reputation as secure and impregnable as that? Ella becomes impatient when efforts are made to analyse her work. 'Listen brother, I sure get all shook up when folks start theorizing about my singing. I just tell 'em to sit back and relax. Yeah, that's it, relax. I just sing as I feel, man. Jazz ain't intellectual.'

But Ella is not a jazz singer. Not in the way that Billie Holiday was a jazz singer. And yet jazz is the source of everything she does. Carmen McRae, younger than Ella and a fervent admirer, describes her singing as 'the epitome of jazz feeling and the popular song wedded together. With her, the transition from jazz to the commercial context wasn't only smooth, it was artistic.'

Neither is she a blues singer, as Bessie Smith was. Speaking of blues singers, Dizzy Gillespie remarked, 'Ella Fitzgerald can't do it; I've never heard Ella Fitzgerald do it.' Nor is she in the tradition of the gospel or soul singers, as Mahalia Jackson and Aretha Franklin are.

Although she was born in the South, Ella Fitzgerald is a child of city streets; the first music she heard came out of a radio loudspeaker and the turntable of a wind-up gramophone. 'My mother,' she says, 'had records of Mamie Smith, the Mills Brothers, the Boswell Sisters and all. I'd listen to them and Connee Boswell became my favourite.' Music for her was the popular song of the moment; the tin pan alley outpourings that were in the very air she breathed. To this was wedded the use being made of such music by the bold and brassy big bands of Harlem in the early thirties. Fletcher Henderson, Benny Carter and Chick Webb. And the way the Lindy-hoppers danced at the Savoy. 'The beat, Ella,' as Chick would urge her. 'Always go with the beat.'

It was the bands who made the singers in those days. Seated among the musicians night after night, how could they not learn the language? Peggy Lee with Benny Goodman, Sarah Vaughan with Earl Hines, Lena Horne with Charlie Barnet. Ella Fitzgerald with Chick Webb. David Weiss in the Los Angeles *Herald Examiner*: 'The bottom line is, she's just another "cat", a working musician whose concentration on sound and phrasing detail lets you know she absorbed the top-drawer stylists from Louis Armstrong to Lester Young to Charlie Parker. Absorbed them? She's *one* of them.'

But all of that fails to explain such extraordinary staying power. What must be added is that remarkable instrument, her voice. Of exceptional range, almost three octaves, and with impeccable intonation and dazzling flexibility, it has changed hardly at all through the years. Derek Jewell, reviewing Ella's appearance at Ronnie Scott's club in London in 1974, wrote: 'Her voice has lost a little of its sweetness; it has more smokiness now.' And Whitney Balliet at a Carnegie Hall concert in 1978: 'Some of her lower tones have more resonance now, and her middle register has thickened, but her voice is still a teenager's – light, pure, boxy, emotionless.'

The absence of emotion, noted by Balliet, is not meant pejoratively. A part of her uniqueness is that she has always set the melodic line of a song above any meaning the words might happen to possess – another example of her musician-like approach to her work. It is also a legacy of her earliest years as a recording artist, when A and R men and managers were dictating which songs she was to sing, and when most of those songs were either leftovers from the available repertoire, or else, were songs deemed fit only for the 'race record' catalogue. One of the first titles she recorded (in 1936), was a song called 'Shine'.

> Just because my hair is curly,
> Just because my teeth are pearly;
> Just because I always wear a smile,
> Like to dress up in the latest style...

Such a song, with its images of the happy-go-lucky laughing Negro (composed, one is surprised to learn, by black writers, Ford Dabney and Cecil Mack), would be unthinkable today, but in the 30s, when black artists were expected to perpetuate whitey's stereotyped model of their life-style, they were all the rage. Of Louis Armstrong, who recorded the same song, most memorably, in 1931, Billie Holiday once fondly remarked, 'I love Pops. He Uncle Toms straight from the heart.'

Dave Frishberg, songwriter and composer, speaking to Kitty Grime (*Jazz Voices*), said, 'A lot of people say that Ella Fitzgerald doesn't sing with meaning, that she doesn't understand what she's singing. Yet, when I listen to her sing that song book series – these are the definitive versions. Maybe it's because she *doesn't* attempt to imbue each line with special meanings and everything, she's just treating it as a musical phrase to be sung in a musical and economical way, the *song* comes right across.'

Since 1954, when Norman Granz became her personal manager, and she began to be treated with the respect that she deserved, Ella has chosen her material with discernment, over an enormously wide range. Fashion has influenced her choices hardly at all. She has lived and worked through tremendous upheavals in the world of popular music; from the great black bands of Harlem, through the rise and fall of the bands of the swing era, through the golden years of Broadway musical theatre, through bebop, rhythm and blues, rock 'n' roll and heavy metal rock, and from each she has selected the best. 'We don't have the Cole Porters and the George Gershwins anymore, but we do have the Burt Bacharachs, Stevie Wonder and people like Paul Williams. I dig his lyrics. I also dig Marvin Gaye. When I sang his "What's Goin' On?" some people said, "Why are you doing that? It's a protest song!" I told them, "I don't find it that way. To me it's good music."'

Ella Fitzgerald *is* good music.

ELLA FITZGERALD:
A SELECTIVE DISCOGRAPHY

Ella Fitzgerald Golden Greats: including *A-Tisket, A-Tasket*, with Chick Webb; *Into Each Life Some Rain Must Fall*, with the Ink Spots; *Stairway To The Stars*; *It's Only A Paper Moon*; *Basin Street Blues*; *My One And Only Love*, with Ellis Larkins; *I've Got The World On A String*; *Walkin' By The River*; *Lover Come Back To Me*; *Mixed Emotions*; *Smooth Sailing*; *You'll Have To Swing It*; *I Wished On The Moon*; *That Old Black Magic*, with Benny Carter; *It's Too Soon To Know*; *The Tender Trap*. With various bands from 1938–55.

MCA MCM 5009

Ella And Ellis including **Ella Sings Gershwin**: *Nice Work If You Can Get It*; *Someone To Watch Over Me*; *My One And Only*; *But Not For Me*; *I've Got A Crush On You*; *Soon*. Ella Fitzgerald and Ellis Larkins (piano).

MCA MCL 1775

Jazz At The Philharmonic: The Ella Fitzgerald Set: *My Bill*; *Why Don't You Do Right*; *A Foggy Day*; *The Man That Got Away*; *Hernando's Hideaway*, Ella Fitzgerald and her trio: Raymond Tunia (piano), Ray Brown (bass), Buddy Rich (drums). *Black Coffee*; *Somebody Loves Me*; *Basin Street Blues*, with the Hank Jones trio: Hank Jones (piano), Ray Brown (bass), Buddy Rich (drums). *Flying Home*, with the JATP All Stars: Roy Eldridge (trumpet), Tommy Turk (trombone), Charlie Parker (alto sax), Lester Young (tenor), Flip Phillips (tenor), Hank Jones (piano), Ray Brown (bass), Buddy Rich (drums).

Verve 815147–1

The Cole Porter Songbook: *All Through The Night*; *Anything Goes*; *Miss Otis Regrets*; *Too Darn Hot*; *In The Still Of The Night*; *I Get A Kick Out Of You*; *Do I Love You*; *Always True To You In My Fashion*; *Let's Do It*; *Just One Of Those Things*; *Ev'ry Time We Say Goodbye*; *All Of You*; *Begin The Beguine*; *Get Out Of Town*; *I Am In Love*; *From This Moment On*; *I Love Paris*; *You Do Something To Me*; *Ridin' High*; *Easy To Love*; *It's All Right With Me*; *Why Can't You Behave*; *What Is This Thing Called Love*; *You're The Top*; *Love For Sale*; *It's Delovely*; *Night And Day*; *Ace In The Hole*; *So In Love*; *I've Got You Under My Skin*; *I Concentrate On You*; *Don't Fence Me In*. With the Buddy Bregman orchestra.

Verve 2683044 1956

Ella Fitzgerald Sings The Rodgers And Hart Songbook: *Have You Met Miss Jones*; *You Took Advantage Of Me*; *A Ship Without A Sail*; *To Keep My Love Alive*; *Dancing On The Ceiling*; *The Lady Is A Tramp*; *With A Song In My Heart*; *Manhattan*; *Johnny One Note*; *I Wish I Were In Love Again*; *Spring*

143

Is Here; It Never Entered My Mind; This Can't Be Love; Thou Swell; My Romance; Where Or When; Little Girl Blue; Give It Back To The Indians; Ten Cents A Dance; There's A Small Hotel; I Didn't Know What Time It Was; Ev'rything I've Got; I Could Write A Book; Blue Room; My Funny Valentine; Bewitched; Mountain Greenery; Wait Till You See Her; Lover: Isn't It Romantic; Here In My Arms; Blue Moon; My Heart Stood Still; I've Got Five Dollars. With the Buddy Bregman orchestra.

Verve   2–2519 1956

Ella And Louis: *Can't We Be Friends; Isn't It A Lovely Day; Moonlight In Vermont; They Can't Take That Away From Me; Under A Blanket Of Blue; Tenderly; A Foggy Day; Stars Fell On Alabama; Cheek To Cheek; The Nearness of You.* With Louis Armstrong and the Oscar Peterson quartet: Oscar Peterson (piano), Herb Ellis (guitar), Ray Brown (bass), Buddy Rich (drums).

Verve   235070 1956

Porgy And Bess: *Summertime; I Wants To Stay Here; Ma Man's Gone Now; I Got Plenty O' Nuttin'; The Buzzard Song; Bess You Is My Woman Now; It Ain't Necessarily So; What You Want Wid Bess; A Woman Is A Sometime Thing; Oh Doctor Jesus; Here Come De Honey Man; Crab Man; Oh Dey's So Fresh And Fine; There's A Boat Dat's Leavin' Soon For New York; Oh Bess Oh Where's My Bess; Oh Lawd I'm On My Way.* With Louis Armstrong and Russell Garcia's orchestra.

Verve   2–2507 1957

Ella And Louis Again Vol. 1: *Don't Be That Way; Makin' Whoopee; They All Laughed; Comes Love; Autumn In New York; Let's Do It; Stompin' At The Savoy; I Won't Dance; Gee Baby Ain't I Good To You.* With Louis Armstrong and the Oscar Peterson quartet: Oscar Peterson (piano), Herb Ellis (guitar), Ray Brown (bass), Louis Bellson (drums).

Verve   2304501 1957

Ella Fitzgerald Sings The Irving Berlin Song Book: *Let's Face The Music And Dance; You're Laughing At Me; Let Yourself Go; You Can Have Him; Russian Lullaby; Puttin' On The Ritz; Get Thee Behind Me Satan; Alexander's Ragtime Band; Top Hat, White Tie And Tails; How About Me; Cheek To Cheek; I Used To Be Colour Blind; How Deep Is The Ocean; All By Myself; Remember; Blue Skies; Suppertime; How's Chances; Heat Wave; Isn't This A Lovely Day; You Keep Coming Back Like A Song; Reaching For The Moon; Slumming On Park Avenue; The Song Is Ended; I'm Putting All My Eggs In One Basket; Now It Can Be Told; Always; It's A Lovely Day Today; Change Partners; No Strings; I've Got My Love To Keep Me Warm.* With Paul Weston's orchestra.   Verve   2683027 1958

The George And Ira Gershwin Songbook: *The Man I Love; A Foggy Day; Oh Lady Be Good; Nice Work If You Can Get It; They All Laughed; Who Cares; Love Is Here To Stay; 'Swonderful; Lorelei; Fascinating Rhythm; Soon; I've Got A Crush On You; Bidin' My Time; Of Thee I Sing; I Got Rhythm; That Certain Feeling; The Half Of It Deary Blues; My Cousin In Milwaukee; I Can't Be Bothered Now; Embraceable You; They Can't Take That Away From Me; Clap Yo' Hands; Things Are Looking Up; By Strauss; Someone To Watch Over Me; Isn't It A Pity; Shall We Dance; But Not For Me; You've Got What Gets Me; Let's Call The Whole Thing Off.* With the Nelson Riddle orchestra.   Verve   2–2525 1959

144

Mack The Knife – Ella In Berlin: *Gone With The Wind; Misty; The Lady Is A Tramp; The Man I Love; Summertime; Too Darn Hot; Lorelei; Mack The Knife; How High The Moon.* With the Peterson quartet.

Verve 2304 155 1960

Ella In Hollywood – Recorded Live At The Crescendo: *This Could Be The Start Of Something Big; I've Got The World On A String; You're Driving Me Crazy; Just In Time; It Might As Well Be Spring; Take The 'A' Train; Stairway To The Stars; Mr Paganini; Satin Doll; Blue Moon; Baby Won't You Please Come Home; Air Mail Special.* Ella Fitzgerald and her quintet: Jim Hall (guitar), Lou Levy (piano), Wilfred Middlebrooks (bass), Gus Johnson (drums).

Verve V6 4052 1961

Rhythm Is My Business: *Rough Ridin'; Broadway; You Can Depend On Me; Runnin' Wild; Show Me The Way To Go Out Of This World; I'll Always Be In Love With You; Hallelujah I Love Him So; I Can't Face The Music; No Moon At All; Laughin' On The Outside; After You've Gone.* With the Bill Doggett orchestra.

Verve 2304558 1962

On The Sunny Side Of The Street: *Honeysuckle Rose; 'Deed I Do; Into Each Life Some Rain Must Fall; Them There Eyes; Dream A Little Dream Of Me; Tea For Two; Satin Doll; I'm Beginning To See The Light; Shiny Stockings; My Last Affair; Ain't Misbehavin'; On The Sunny Side Of The Street.* With Count Basie and his orchestra.

Verve 2304049 1963

Ella And Duke On The Côte D'Azur: *It Don't Mean A Thing; Mack The Knife; Squeeze Me; Jazz Samba; Going Out Of My Head; Misty; Lullaby Of Birdland; How Long Has This Been Going On; The More I See You.* With Duke Ellington and his orchestra.

Verve 711 055

Ella À Nice: *Night And Day; Get Out Of Town; Easy To Love; You Do Something To Me; Body And Soul; The Man I Love; Porgy; The Girl From Ipanema; Fly Me To The Moon; O Nosso Amor; Cielito Lindo; Magdalena; Agua De Beber; Summertime; They Can't Take That Away From Me; Mood Indigo; Do Nothin' Till You Hear From Me; It Don't Mean A Thing; Something; St Louis Blues; Close To You; Put A Little Love In Your Heart.* With the Tommy Flanagan trio: Tommy Flanagan (piano), Frank De La Rosa (bass), Ed Thigpen (drums).

Pablo 2308234 1971

Take Love Easy: *Take Love Easy; Once I Loved; Don't Be That Way; You're Blasé; Lush Life; A Foggy Day In London Town; Gee Baby Ain't I Good To You; You Go To My Head; I Want To Talk About You.* With Joe Pass (guitar).

Pablo 2310702 1973

Ella In London: *Sweet Georgia Brown; They Can't Take That Away From Me; Every Time We Say Goodbye; The Man I Love; It Don't Mean A Thing If It Ain't Got That Swing; You've Got A Friend; Lemon Drop; The Very Thought Of You; Happy Blues.* With the Tommy Flanagan quartet: Tommy Flanagan (piano), Joe Pass (guitar), Keter Betts (bass), Bobby Durham (drums).

Pablo 2310711 1974

Fine And Mellow: *Fine And Mellow; I'm Just A Lucky So And So; I Don't Stand The Ghost Of A Chance With You; Rockin' In Rhythm; I'm In The Mood For Love; 'Round Midnight; I Can't Give You Anything But Love; The Man I Love; Polka Dots And Moonbeams.* Ella Fitzgerald Jam: Harry Edison (trumpet), Clark Terry (trumpet), Zoot Sims (tenor sax), Eddie Lockjaw Davis (tenor sax), Joe Pass (guitar), Tommy Flanagan (piano), Ray Brown (bass), Louis Bellson (drums).

Pablo 2310829 1974

Ella – At The Montreux Jazz Festival 1975: *Caravan; Satin Doll; Teach Me Tonight; It's All Right With Me; Let's Do It; How High The Moon; The Girl From Ipanema; 'Tain't Nobody's Business.* With the Tommy Flanagan trio: Tommy Flanagan (piano), Keter Betts (bass), Bobby Durham (drums).

Pablo 2310751 1975

Fitzgerald And Pass – Again: *I Ain't Got Nothin' But The Blues; 'Tis Autumn; My Old Flame; That Old Feeling; Rain; I Didn't Know About You; You Took Advantage Of Me; I've Got The World On A String; All Too Soon; The One I Love Belongs To Somebody Else; Solitude; Nature Boy; Tennessee Waltz; One Note Samba.* With Joe Pass (guitar).

Pablo 2310772 1976

Lady Time: *I'm Walkin'; All Or Nothing At All; I Never Had A Chance; I Cried For You; What Will I Tell My Heart; Since I Fell For You; And The Angels Sing; I'm Confessin'; Mack The Knife; That's My Desire; I'm In The Mood For Love.* With Jackie Davis (organ), Louis Bellson (drums).

Pablo 2310 825 1978

A Perfect Match – Basie And Ella: *Please Don't Talk About Me When I'm Gone; Sweet Georgia Brown; Some Other Spring; Make Me Rainbows; After You've Gone; Round About Midnight; Fine and Mellow; You've Changed; Honeysuckle Rose; St Louis Blues.* With the Count Basie orchestra.

Pablo 2312110 Digital 1979

Ella Abraca Jobim: *Somewhere In The Hills; The Girl From Ipanema; Dindi; Desafinado; Wave; Agua De Beber; Triste; How Insensitive; He's A Carioca; Don't Ever Go Away; A Felicidade; This Love That I've Found; Dreamer; Corcovado; Song Of The Jet; Bonita; One Note Samba; Useless Landscape.* With Orchestra: Clark Terry (trumpet), Zoot Sims (tenor sax), Toots Thielmans (harmonica), Joe Pass (guitar), Oscar Castro-neves (guitar), Paul Jackson (guitar), Mitch Holder (guitar), Roland Bautista (guitar), Terry Trotter (keyboards), Mike Lang (keyboards), Clarence McDonald (keyboards), Abe Laboriel (bass), Alejandro Neciosup Acuna (drums), Paulinho Da Costa (percussion), Erich Bulling (arranger, conductor).

Pablo 2630201 1980

Nice Work If You Can Get It: With André Previn and his orchestra. *A Foggy Day; Nice Work If You Can Get It; But Not For Me; Let's Call The Whole Thing Off; How Long Has This Been Going On; Who Cares; Medley: I've Got A Crush On You, Someone To Watch Over Me, Embraceable You; The Can't Take That Away From Me.*

Pablo Today K12-40

BIBLIOGRAPHY

Anderson, Jervis: *Harlem, the Great Black Way 1900–1950* (Orbis, 1982)

Berendt, Joachim E.: *The Jazz Book* (Granada, 1983)

Balliet, Whitney: *Night Creature* (Oxford, New York, 1981)

Balliet, Whitney: *Such Sweet Thunder* (Macdonald, 1968)

Cerulli, Dom, Korell, Burt and Nasatir, Mort: *The Jazz World* (Ballantine Books, New York, 1960)

Collier, James Lincoln: *Louis Armstrong* (Michael Joseph, 1984)

Chilton, John: *Billie's Blues* (Quartet, 1975)

Durante, Jimmy and Kofoed, Jack: *Night Clubs* (Knopf, New York, 1931)

Dahl, Linda: *Stormy Weather* (Quartet, 1984)

Ellington, Duke: *Music is my Mistress* (W. H. Allen, 1974)

Ellison, Ralph: *Invisible Man* (Gollancz, 1953)

Feather, Leonard: *The Encyclopedia of Jazz* (Quartet, 1978)

Feather, Leonard: *From Satchmo to Miles* (Quartet, 1974)

Fox, Ted: *Showtime at the Apollo* (Holt, Rinehart & Winston, New York, 1983)

Gillespie, Dizzy: *To Be Or Not To Bop* (W. H. Allen, 1980)

Grime, Kitty: *Jazz Voices* (Quartet, 1983)

Hammond, John: *John Hammond on Record* (Ridge Press, New York, 1977)

Haskins, James: *The Cotton Club* (Robson Books, 1985)

Haskins, James, with Kathleen Benson: *Lena* (Stein & Day, New York, 1984).

Jewell, Derek: *The Popular Voice* (Deutsch, 1980)

Jones, Max and Chilton, John: *Louis* (Stein & Day, New York, 1984)

Jepsen, Jorgen: *Jazz Records, 1942–1968* (Knudsen, Copenhagen, 1963–1970)

Krivine, J.: *Juke Box Saturday Night* (New English Library, 1977)

Lewis, David Levering: *When Harlem was in Vogue* (Knopf, New York, 1981)

McCarthy, Albert: *Big Band Jazz* (Barrie & Jenkins, 1974)

Palmer, Richard: *Oscar Peterson* (Spellmount, 1984)

Rodgers, Richard: *Musical Stages* (Random House, New York, 1975)

Spaeth, Sigmund: *A History of Popular Music in America* (Random House, New York, 1948)

Shaw, Artie: *The Trouble with Cinderella* (Farrar, Straus & Young, New York, 1952)

Shapiro, Nat and Hentoff, Nat: *Hear Me Talkin' To You* (Rinehart & Co., New York, 1955)

Terkel, Studs: *Hard Times* (Allen Lane, 1970)

Wells, Dickie (as told to Stanley Dance): *The Night People* (Robert Hale, 1971)

INDEX

148